GRA   **Gray, Sherilee.**
       Crashed

FRA

2015

crashed

an *Axle Alley Vipers* novel

D1527241

Sherilee Gray

ST. MARY PARISH LIBRARY
FRANKLIN, LOUISIANA

This book is a work of fiction. Names, characters, places, and incidents are the product of the author's imagination or are used fictitiously. Any resemblance to actual events, locales, or persons, living or dead, is coincidental.

Copyright © 2015 by Sherilee Gray. All rights reserved, including the right to reproduce, distribute, or transmit in any form or by any means. For information regarding subsidiary rights, please contact the Publisher.

Entangled Publishing, LLC
2614 South Timberline Road
Suite 109
Fort Collins, CO 80525
Visit our website at www.entangledpublishing.com.

Indulgence is an imprint of Entangled Publishing, LLC.

Edited by Karen Grove
Cover design by Liz Pelletier
Cover art by iStock

Manufactured in the United States of America

First Edition July 2015

ST. MARY PARISH LIBRARY
FRANKLIN, LOUISIANA

For my mother.
Thank you for being awesome. x

Chapter One

Alex Franco planted her ass on a chair that was about as comfortable as a slab of concrete—but no doubt cost more than every piece of furniture in her apartment combined—and pretended to inspect her fingernails. Every pair of eyes in the stylish reception area of West Enterprises had now shifted to her. She knew this because she could feel them like laser beams burning a hole into the top of her head.

Whatever. Wasn't the first time, wouldn't be the last.

She glanced down at her beaten-to-hell work boots and shifted her foot to cover the black grease mark she'd tracked into the carpet, then scowled for giving a shit.

Right then, she didn't have it in her to feel bad for staining Deacon West's very expensive carpet. Served the jackass right.

Drying her sweaty palms on the sides of her shorts, she sat back and crossed her arms. God, this was the last place she wanted to be right now. Fridays were busy at the garage.

Three cars were booked in for this afternoon, a new record for them. She didn't have time for this.

Another woman dressed in a pencil skirt and pumps walked in and parked it beside her buddy already sitting behind the oversize reception desk. Did they all dress the same on purpose? Or was it some weird, unspoken law?

The two of them immediately started whispering and giggling. Alex lifted her gaze, narrowing her eyes on the pair of Stepford wife clone-factory rejects. The bitches were looking at her like she was something from another goddamned planet.

Morons.

She could only guess the reason security hadn't shown up and dragged her out already was because they were hoping for a free show. And the only reason she was stuck out here cooling her heels, and not tearing Deacon a new one, was because the bastard had his office door locked.

She tightened her fingers around the letter in her hand. How could he do this to his sisters? Piper and Rusty loved their brother, trusted him. They'd be devastated if they knew what he was up to behind their backs. She didn't want to believe he would sell their garage out from under them, but why else would he want the building valued? Alex had met the West girls when she was just ten years old. They'd quickly become best friends—her lifeline. This could tear them apart, could tear apart the business they'd been working so hard to keep afloat, to make a success. She couldn't let that happen—she wouldn't.

She shifted in her seat when another leggy blonde sauntered past and tried not to feel self-conscious. Not easy when her tank and cutoffs were grease stained and her hair was a mess.

God, she hadn't thought this through, had let her temper get the better of her. Again. Maybe she should just get the hell out of here. Call the asshat instead to give him a piece of her mind. This really didn't need to be done in person, right?

It had been six long months, but she realized, in that moment, she still wasn't ready to see him.

Crap.

Retreat! Regroup! Run like hell!

She stood and spun on the grubby soles of her boots, getting his carpet good and filthy before she bolted toward the elevators. She'd managed two steps when she heard the click of a door opening behind her.

"Alex?"

Ah, shit. She took another retreating step.

"Stop right there."

That familiar voice moved through her, the rough command hitting her low in the belly, lifting goose bumps on her bare arms.

There was no way she could run now and keep her dignity intact. Planting her hands on her hips, she took a deep breath and mentally prepared herself for the devastation that seeing Deacon again would bring.

Then spun around.

Goddammit.

The oxygen rushed from her lungs. Yep, the guy was still as hot as he'd been six months ago. Maybe hotter, if that were possible. It was all still there in mouthwatering abundance. The broad shoulders. The long legs. The rugged good looks and piercing green eyes. That melt-your-panties dimple in his chin.

But what always got to her, the thing that made her chest tight and had the ability to make her forget what a giant asshole he'd become, was the overlong hair. It brushed the collar of his shirt, in need of a serious trim, too long, too casual for the man he was now. That hair belonged on the scruffy teen who'd worked in his father's garage after school and on weekends. That hair did not belong on Mr. Businessman of the Year.

She let her gaze travel to the reason his office door had been locked in the middle of the day, the tall blonde dangling off his arm like a cheap handbag. Alex bit her lip when the familiar pain socked her in the chest.

Harden the hell up, Franco. What? You think he's been a monk all these months?

The guy was rich and incredibly good-looking. He could screw whoever he liked, as often as he liked. And apparently during the day in his office wasn't off-limits.

His gaze moved over her body, but his face gave nothing away. Her palms got sweaty again, and her heart started to pound harder.

"Well, this is a surprise. To what do I owe this rare pleasure?" She didn't miss the hint of bitterness in his voice, because the bastard wasn't trying to hide it.

The blonde hadn't retracted her claws from his arm and looked Alex up and down like she was something the rodent-sized, froufrou dog she no doubt had at home had just dragged in.

"You know why I'm here, Deke. So cut the bullshit." Gasps came from the receptionists, whose heads were so close together now they could pass as conjoined twins, and Deacon's blonde narrowed her eyes like she wanted to scratch Alex's eyes out of her head.

The blonde turned into him and smashed her impressive breasts into his side. "Who is this, Deacon? We're supposed to be having lunch." She batted what had to be false lashes and pouted her bee-stung pink lips like a blowup doll.

Alex snorted, couldn't help herself. The woman was a walking, talking cliché.

Deacon tried to hide it, but she didn't miss the way he tensed, or the way that muscle in his jaw jumped several times. He was clenching his teeth — he did that when he was annoyed, always had. She tried to shrug it off. So he was pissed she'd ruined his lunch date. Well, tough shit.

What did she expect? That the guy had woken up one day and *boom*, he was no longer a complete and utter asshole? That her feelings would have magically disappeared? If only life were that simple. Her feelings hadn't diminished, not one tiny bit in all these years. She should have known better, should have left this for Piper or Rusty to sort out.

Deacon disentangled the woman from his arm and took a step back. "Apologies. We'll have to make it another time, Candice." And just like that he dismissed the handbag.

Candice's lips thinned. "You have got to be kidding me?"

He pinned her with a look Alex had never seen before and thankfully had never been the recipient of. God, she almost felt sorry for her.

Almost.

"We'll catch up another time."

Blondie stared at him openmouthed for several seconds, then with a huff, flicked her long mane over her shoulder and flounced out of the office.

She noted Deacon didn't watch his date leave, his gaze remained firmly pinned on her. He stepped back and held the door open for her without a word. When she hesitated, the pissed-off vibe he was already throwing ratcheted up a notch. "You're here to see me, right?"

She didn't bother answering and stomped forward, sliding past him into his office. *Too late to back out now.*

The room was big, fancy as hell, decked out with all the best crap money could buy. Massive windows covered half the wall space, giving him a spectacular view overlooking the city of Miami. He'd more than likely gazed out at that view while he banged the human Barbie over his desk. She forced those thoughts from her mind. Deacon's sordid sex life was none of her business.

Crossing her arms, needing a barrier, no matter how flimsy, she turned to face him. It didn't matter how many times she saw him like this, she still had a hard time reconciling this Deacon in his power suits and big office with the boy who'd helped out in his father's garage to save for college.

She looked around, took it all in, and her belly clenched. He'd gotten everything he'd ever wanted. He was a self-made man, a success at only twenty-eight years old, just three years older than her. Too young to be so damn cynical.

God, she still mourned the boy he'd been, the one she'd fallen for when she was just fourteen. The boy she'd trailed after like a lost puppy. Unrequited love at its most pathetic. He'd been her knight in grease-stained coveralls, been there for her more times than she could count.

She didn't know this Deacon, didn't know if she wanted to.

"What the hell happened to you?" The words slipped

past her lips before she could engage her brain.

His jaw hardened, and the muscle jumped again. "I could ask you the same thing."

"Jesus. Forget it." She'd been in the same room with him for less than a minute, and already they were bitching at each other.

His wide shoulders stiffened as he walked to his desk, then rested his ass on its surface. "Why are you here, Alex? I have work to do and now, thanks to you, I won't get lunch."

Ouch.

She ignored the coldness in his voice, the way his displeasure at seeing her made her want to crawl into the nearest hole and curl into the fetal position, and focused on her anger. She slammed the now rumpled letter on the desk beside him. "What the hell's this?"

He glanced down but didn't pick it up. His expression didn't change, remained smooth and unaffected. "I own that building, which includes the garage and the apartment you live in upstairs. As your landlord, I'm only required to give you forty-eight hours' notice to enter your apartment. You're lucky I decided to be generous and give you two weeks before I brought the valuer in."

She gritted her teeth. "Why the goddamned valuer, Deke? Are you selling the garage out from under us?"

He shrugged. "I'm thinking about it."

Her stomach flipped; she hadn't wanted to believe it. She curled her fingers into tight fists, fighting back the hurt and the feeling of betrayal. Fear settled in the pit of her stomach, heavy and cold. "How could you do that to your own sisters?" *How could you do that to me?* "Have you told Piper or Rusty you plan on selling our livelihood out from underneath us?"

"It's time to stop playing shop, Alex. The sooner I get rid of that place, the sooner my sisters can move on with their lives."

She couldn't believe what she was hearing. "That garage *is* our lives. Me, Piper, and Rusty. It was a big part of yours once, too."

He didn't react.

So damn cold.

"You're a good mechanic. You'll find another job easy enough."

"My God, Deacon. Do they remove your heart when you graduate business school?"

He laughed, the sound so bitter it chilled her to the bone. "I wish."

Alex tried to think fast—she had to stop this. They couldn't lose everything they'd worked so hard to build. "When your dad died, he left the business to us...he wanted—"

"But he left the building to me."

"—to make sure your sisters always had security." The bastard must love this, love making her beg. "Give us time to prove we can do this. We can make it work."

The business had been a thriving one, but after Deacon's dad died, they'd lost customers. Men who thought girls made crappy mechanics decided to take their business elsewhere. "We just need a bit more time to build a new client base."

"Don't you think you've had long enough? How long has it been? Since we buried Dad? Hmm, let me see, six months?" His voice was so emotionless it sent shivers down her spine.

He knew exactly how long it had been. Like he could forget the date of his father's funeral. Her face heated, and she dropped her gaze from his, unable to hold it any longer.

Not when images best forgotten filled her mind. The way his powerful body had strained above hers, the sounds he'd made as he'd pounded into her, the look on his face right before he'd come, the way he'd trembled in her arms afterward.

The way he'd looked sleeping right before she crept out of his room without so much as a *see you around*. The worst part was, she'd wanted to stay—God, so much—but she'd already been there, done that. She knew what staying would have gotten her—another dose of heartache and humiliation. Something she actively tried to avoid.

When she was eighteen, after years of wishing he'd love her back, Deke had finally made a move. Believing he was *the one*, she'd fallen all over him like the desperate idiot she'd been. But he'd made it clear she wasn't the type of woman you settled down with. No, she was the type of woman you fucked and left behind. Which made falling back into bed with him again, six months ago, all the more stupid.

She shivered, hated that despite everything, she still wanted him. Her heart squeezed, body heating like it always did around him. "I know how long it's been," she rasped.

A hard smile turned up the corners of his lips. "I thought you might've forgotten." He pushed away from the desk and walked right up to her, invading her personal space. Suddenly trapped in his force field, she was unable to step back. "Maybe I've been wrong all these months. Maybe you haven't forgotten after all. Have you thought of that night, Alex? Thought about how good we were together?" His gaze darkened. "What it was like to have my mouth on you, my cock moving inside you?"

Oh, God, she had. Every goddamned night since. She shivered, a delicious ache building steadily between her thighs. He wasn't playing fair. The bastard knew how much she loved his dirty mouth, how much it turned her on. How she loved it when he used that impressive body to corner her, pin her down, take control.

He smirked, reading her so easily. "That's what I thought."

What had she been thinking coming here? Her temper got her into trouble more times than she'd like to admit, but this lack of judgment had to be some kind of new low even for her. She shrugged out of his invisible hold, which wasn't easy, and took a step back. "Wrong. I try to forget my mistakes."

He crossed his arms, creating more distance between them, and shrugged. "You're still that lost little girl, aren't you, Alex? Scared shitless of everything."

What? Her heart pounded, and her breath rushed from her lungs like he'd sucker punched her. "You don't know jack—"

He glanced down, inspected his fingernails, uninterested in what she had to say, and successfully cut her off midsentence without a single word. When he looked up, he said, "Don't you think it's time you grew the hell up?"

She tensed against all that quiet, controlled fury directed at her. And when it came, she welcomed the familiar surge of anger. Getting angry was better than crying. She'd shed more than enough tears over him already. "I'm confused here. Please explain your definition of growing up. Does fucking *you* make me a grown-up? Or just fucking in general?"

His jaw did some more clenching. "You haven't slept with anyone else."

The surety in his tone just pissed her off even more. Dammit, she hated that he was right. She forced a laugh. "What? You think you ruined me for all other men?"

Oh, crap. Wrong thing to say.

He moved back in, so close she could feel the heat of his body against hers. Her traitorous nipples puckered at the contact. He leaned in, his mouth a mere inch from hers, and whispered, "I know I have."

His breath tickled her lips, and despite her anger, she struggled to find the strength to shove him away. "Back the hell up," she ground out.

He didn't budge, gaze dipping to her mouth. She sucked in a breath. He wouldn't, would he? Oh, yeah, it was time to call the men in white coats, because, dammit, she wanted him to, wanted more of those demanding, hungry kisses the man excelled at.

But he stepped back suddenly, and all the air trapped in her lungs came out in a rush. He circled his desk, like he couldn't get away from her fast enough. "I don't have time for your temper tantrums today, Alex."

She was still trying to get her heart rate to slow down and stop her knees from shaking, and he looked unruffled and emotionless. "What are you going to do?"

"I've told you what I'm going to do." He didn't look up from his laptop, dismissing her completely.

"This will kill your sisters." *It's killing* me.

He looked up then and stared at her for a long minute until she wanted to squirm. Instead she scowled.

He picked up a pen and tapped it on the desk. "You really think you can make it work?"

"I know we can." They were getting new clients every week. It was only a matter of time till the place was back in the black.

He leaned back in his chair. "Okay. I'll give you three months." She let out a relieved breath, until he added, "On one condition."

She was almost too afraid to ask. "What is it?"

His gaze moved from her face, across her shoulders, then blazed a heated path over her small breasts and down her belly before lifting to meet hers. "I often need someone to accompany me to functions…"

She ignored her unease and forced an unladylike snort. "You need a date?"

"Yes, but you didn't let me finish." He stayed behind his desk, watching her carefully. "I'm a man, Alex. I have needs like any other. I don't have time for relationships. I don't want a serious commitment, and one-night stands aren't really my thing."

Was he— No way. He couldn't seriously be asking her to be his fuck buddy.

"For the next three months, I want you to fill those roles."

She couldn't believe what she was hearing. "So you're saying…you want…you want me to…"

"I want you to dress up nice, accompany me to dinners and other events I often have to attend. I'll pay for your expenses, of course. Clothes, shoes, salon appointments. Whatever you want." He leaned forward in his chair. "What I'm saying, Alex, is for the next three months, I want you to share my bed. That is what I want."

Her head spun. "You've lost your mind."

He didn't look away; his gaze didn't falter. "Those are my conditions. Nonnegotiable. Take it or leave it."

Still, she stared at him. Waited for him to tell her he was just fucking with her. He didn't. Did he think that little of her? That she was just some dispensable piece of ass? "You have to be joking."

"I'm deadly serious."

She spun and yanked open the door but looked back before she walked out. "I won't be your whore. You can stick your deal."

"Fine. Be ready for the valuer in two weeks."

Chapter Two

Deacon watched Alex storm from his office and cursed.

The impact of seeing her again shouldn't have come as a surprise. She looked just the same. Beautiful. Fucking untouchable.

But as soon as he'd laid eyes on her, those feelings, the ones he'd managed to keep on lockdown, had reared up and sucker punched him in the gut. Along with all the frustration, anger, and disappointment he'd felt waking in that bed alone all those months ago. He'd nearly given in to it. Had been so close to kissing that smart mouth, kissing that maddening attitude right out of her, and forcing her to see exactly what she did to him.

And he would have ruined everything.

Alex acted tough, but she was fractured, brittle. One wrong move, and she'd fall to pieces. Crumble right through his fingers. She'd become so used to pushing everyone away, it was now second nature. She had the don't-mess-with-me attitude, the tattoos. All designed to keep people at arm's length. But he'd tasted the soft, vulnerable woman beneath. And he wouldn't stop till he had more.

Being shipped from one foster family to the next had built that impenetrable wall she hid behind, and it was time to knock it down.

That night with her six months ago, he'd gotten a glimpse of the real Alex again. No way was he letting her go a second time. She'd been there for him after his father died. They'd fallen into bed together, and she'd shown him the beauty that lay beneath the tough exterior, the girl he remembered.

Then he'd woken up to an empty bed. She'd run scared.

He'd tried patient, and he wasn't a patient man. She'd ignored his calls. Avoided him. It didn't matter what he did or said. She wouldn't let him in. That would mean accepting the truth, accepting the way she felt about him, allowing herself to believe that he could actually have feelings for her. She wouldn't willingly expose herself to that kind of pain and heartbreak.

Not again. Not after the way he'd screwed up last time.

Forcing her to confront those feelings now was a risk, but one he had to take. He knew her well enough to know if he tried to sit her down, tell her how he felt about her — she'd run scared. There was no doubt in his mind. And he'd lose her for good.

That couldn't happen.

He was desperate. He was also out of options. If she couldn't figure it out for herself, it was time to clue her in.

She belonged to him. They belonged together.

He'd known she'd come to him all guns blazing when she got his letter, had banked on it. He stood and slipped on his jacket, taking his time going after her. She wasn't going anywhere.

West Restoration, the garage Alex was trying to save—the one he had no intention of selling—was located on Axle Alley. A street in an industrial area, just out of the city, lined with businesses that catered to anything with an engine. In their teens, the local boys had dubbed Alex and Deacon's sisters the Axle Alley Vipers. All three were beautiful, tough in their own way, and if you tried to get too close, tried to touch, they would take a bite out of you.

Jesus. Nothing had changed.

When he got to the parking garage below his building, he saw Martin had done his job. Deacon's car was parked behind Alex's metallic-purple Viper, caging her in.

Her choice of car said more than he thought she realized. Playing up to that moniker, to what it meant, was just another way to keep everyone at a distance, to protect herself.

She stood against the driver's door, arms crossed, more pissed than he'd ever seen her. Her long, shiny brown hair was pulled up in a messy bun that was sexy as hell on her, and those dark, exotic eyes had landed and stayed on him as soon as the elevator doors had opened and he'd stepped out.

His cock twitched under that intense stare.

He allowed his gaze to travel over her. Did she have any idea how stunning she was? The woman could wear a potato sack and still make his dick hard. The intricate rose tattoo decorating the upper half of her right arm drew his eye. It covered a jagged scar you could only see under a certain light, and it moved as she shoved her hands in her pockets, flexing her finely honed bicep. "This your doing?" she asked.

He kept on walking toward her. She tensed as he came

closer, but he didn't stop until he was close enough to smell her vanilla scent, hear her subtle exhale as he leaned in. "You were in my parking spot."

Fire flashed in her eyes. "Bullshit. What about the other ten free spots?"

He shrugged. "I like this one."

She blew out a frustrated breath. "If you're so damned attached to this one, let me out and you can have it back."

He reached out, ran the tip of his finger along that scar. It curved around a rose petal, then joined a thorny stem. He felt her tremble. Jesus, he loved that, loved how easily he affected her. "Let's stop playing games. This isn't about a parking spot, and you know it."

"I said no." Her voice shook and her breathing quickened.

"I won't accept that answer. Not yet." *Not ever.* "I want you to think about it first. Really think about it. We're good together. Tell me you've had better. Because I haven't."

She sucked in a shaky breath. "You were grieving. Your perception is skewed."

It took all his strength not to kiss her. "Yes, I was grieving. But that wasn't the only reason we ended up in bed together, and you know it. You wanted me, and I sure as hell wanted you. Still do. It's really as simple as that."

And if he was wrong, if she didn't return his feelings? He'd walk away. It would kill him to do it, but despite what he'd said to her, they both knew he'd never force her into a relationship, sexual or otherwise. Not ever.

She hugged herself. "Why are you doing this? And why now, after all this time?"

He noted she didn't deny what he'd said, didn't deny wanting him. *Thank fuck.* "Why have you avoided me for six months?" he asked instead of answering her.

She bit her lip. "I haven't."

"You're full of it."

"Move your damn car. We're busy at work, and I need to get back."

"Alex…"

"Let me go, Deke."

Not going to happen. He'd done it once, and it had been the biggest mistake of his life. "Is the idea of spending time with me, of sharing my bed, so distasteful?"

She shook her head. "Can you hear yourself? You've lost it. Jesus. Can you just stop?"

Never. He stepped back. "For now, but I'll be in touch soon."

• • •

Alex leaned her hip against Piper's desk and looked through the partition window out to the workshop. Monday was definitely off to a better start than Friday. She hadn't seen or heard from Deacon over the weekend, but she knew it was only a matter of time.

"What's happening?" Piper asked.

"She's smiling. Our girl's working her magic. Oh, he's going in for the handshake." She squeezed Piper's shoulder. "Holy shit, I think she did it."

Piper did a silent happy dance in her swivel chair and squealed under her breath. "Oh my God, that one job alone will pay for half the new tow truck. And he's talking several big restorations."

The guy turned and left, and Rusty tightened her long

auburn ponytail, spun on her boot, and attempted to walk casually to the office, while grinning like a loon on the verge of busting out in a victory dance.

She walked in and shut the door behind her. All three of them turned to look out the window and watched Mr. Cannon climb into his car and drive away. As soon as his car was out of sight, they all screamed and danced around the office, laughing until tears were running down their faces.

"We did it, bitches!" Rusty flopped down, planting her ass in Piper's chair, and pumped one of her brightly tattooed arms in the air.

"I think the long legs and nice rack can take some of the credit," Piper said, giggling.

"Well, Rusty's rack might have helped us get the job, but when that car drives out of here looking freaking amazing, it will be our talent that has him bringing in the next one. They'll be moving advertisements, ladies," Alex said.

They were at a disadvantage not being set up on South Beach, where all the established big-name car restoration businesses were, but they didn't want to leave Axle Alley. And even if they did, SoBe was way out of their price range. Their only option was to bring the customers to them. And if the novelty of an all-female-run auto repair shop was enough to do that, they'd work it for all it was worth.

Piper grinned, all but busting out of her skin. "This is just the start of the big-money restoration work. It's finally happening." She grabbed Rusty's hand and tugged her out of the chair, then pulled her and Alex in for a group hug. "I wish Dad was here to see this. He'd be so proud of us."

They clung to each other, and Alex's eyes started to sting. Jacob West had been like a father to her, too. She'd loved him and loved this old garage as much as Rusty and Piper did.

She hadn't mentioned her meeting with Deacon. He obviously hadn't told them about his plans to sell the business out from under them yet. God, she was glad she'd kept it to herself. They'd already lost their father, and they loved their brother more than anything. Losing this place would kill them.

She watched the two women who had become her family after her own was taken from her. The excitement on their faces made her chest hurt. How would she ever survive without them, without seeing them every day? Without walking into this place every morning?

In that moment she realized she'd do anything to keep what they had, to keep what they were building. Nothing was more important than these women. She owed them everything. And right then she knew what she had to do. She'd do whatever it took to keep the smiles on their faces, to never lose *this*.

Piper gave them one last squeeze. "You guys close up, and I'll go order the pizza." She did another dance, grabbed her bag, and headed out.

Rusty and Piper lived in a small, quirky cottage next to the garage. It was the only house left on Axle Alley and had once been owned by their grandmother. The West family had lived in it for several generations. Even after their neighbors sold and disappeared, and new commercial buildings took their place, Grandma West had refused to sell. She'd left it to her granddaughters, who were just as determined to keep it as it was, despite the constant barrage of offers they received to take it off their hands. But it didn't matter how much the land was worth. It wasn't for sale.

They shut up shop, and Alex headed to her apartment above the garage. After a quick shower, she pulled on her comfy jeans with all the rips and her favorite Metallica T-shirt, leaving her long hair down to dry naturally. Then, before she could talk herself out of it, she grabbed her phone and texted Deacon.

We need to talk. I'll call you later.

Shoving her phone back in her pocket, she headed next door to the cottage for celebratory pizza. She refused to think about the agreement she was about to enter into, or what it would mean for her. Not yet.

When she hit the stairs to the cottage, she heard music coming from inside, laughter, and even with all this Deacon crap hanging over her head, she couldn't stop the smile that spread across her face. She walked into the living room, and three beers sat open on the coffee table. Rusty came dancing from the kitchen, carrying a bag of potato chips and a tub of dip.

Her friend grinned. "We're celebrating, baby. We'll worry about the size of our asses tomorrow."

Alex laughed. "Nothing wrong with some junk in the trunk."

"You said it." Rusty spun around and gave her perfect, round ass a wiggle.

Piper followed with the pizza, and they sat, ate, laughed, and made plans for the garage. Something they hadn't done in a while, too afraid to get their hopes up, afraid they'd fail. But with business picking up, they could afford to dream again, not to mention buy extravagant things like chips and dip.

No, it didn't matter how Alex looked at it—her decision had been made for her. There had never been any other choice. Her life here with Piper and Rusty meant *everything* to her. She couldn't—wouldn't—lose it.

Her stomach fluttered. Christ, now she just had to tell Deacon.

She chugged back the rest of her third beer, happy for the buzz and the Dutch courage, and stood. Time to make the call, get it over with before she chickened out or sobered up. "Okay. I'm heading off. We can't make money if we're all hungover in the morning, right?"

The other two groaned. "All right, but this Friday, it's girls' night. We're going out, and we're gonna drink too much and shake it on the dance floor," Rusty said, then downed the rest of her beer.

Weekend plans made, Alex left the cottage and crossed the parking lot to her place. It was dark out, and she almost missed the silver Mercedes S 600 parked behind the garage. Almost.

Her step faltered when the door opened and Deke stepped out. He wore dark jeans and a long-sleeved black thermal top that clung to his upper body and made her mouth water. She could see his abs defined through the thin fabric, and it took a huge amount of effort to look away.

"I've been waiting for you," he said.

She was fuzzy from the beers and couldn't muster the energy to be pissed. "Why didn't you come next door?"

"I don't really think this conversation is something you want Piper or Rusty to hear, no?"

No, it isn't.

"Hop in." He held the car door open for her.

She bit her lip. "I told you I was going to call you."

"I decided whatever you have to say, I'd rather hear it in person."

She noticed he kept darting glances at the garage. He looked almost uneasy. Was it painful for him to be here? Yes, she'd avoided Deacon these last few months, but it hadn't been all that hard. He'd barely set foot here since his father's death. All she'd had to do was ignore his calls and texts and make her excuses if she knew Deacon might be at whatever get-together or dinner her friends invited her to.

Maybe there was more to his absence than she'd first thought. She shook her head. "I'd rather do this upstairs."

He hesitated, but she didn't wait for his answer and took the external stairs to her apartment. If being here set off some kind of emotional response in him, it might just break through that cold exterior, and maybe he'd change his mind about selling this place. Maybe he'd remember how important it had been to his family, and at one time to him.

Maybe he'd let her off the hook.

They walked in, and she threw her keys on the coffee table.

Deacon shut the door behind them. "Your text earlier, it was about my offer?"

No beating about the bush then. "Let's get one thing clear here. It's not an offer. An offer implies I have a choice. This is blackmail. Don't kid yourself it's anything else."

His broad shoulders shifted, causing the muscles in his chest to bunch and move in a way that made her belly flip. His eyes narrowed. "You can always say no. No one's holding a gun to your head, Alex."

She snorted. "You sure about that?"

He took a step toward her. "Why are you resisting this? I know you want me." He made a low, rough sound in the back of his throat. "The way you responded to me that night. You haven't forgotten, have you? God, you were so wet, hungry for my cock. You shook so hard when I put my mouth on you, when I nipped your perfect little clit."

A throbbing pulse started between her thighs. Her body still remembered every damn touch, every rough, dirty word he'd whispered in her ear, against her skin. She could almost feel his mouth on her. And just like that, she was wet for him. "It meant nothing." She moved away. "We've already made this mistake before." The beer had loosened her tongue. Jesus, why was she going there now? *Because it still hurts like hell.* "Surely there are other women you can blackmail into screwing you. Why me all of a sudden?"

His hands clenched and unclenched at his sides, his only outward sign of emotion. "First, it doesn't need to *mean* anything. We're talking about sex, Alex, not marriage."

Oh, yeah, that was a low blow considering their history.

"And second, I didn't get nearly enough time with you. Not even close…" She shook her head, afraid of what he'd say next but desperate to hear it all the same. "I want to taste every inch of that hot little body. I want to fuck you every way possible, as often as I like. I want you to come against my mouth, around my fingers, my cock." He sucked in a ragged breath. "Is that a good enough reason for you?"

She took a step back before she realized what she was doing. God, she wanted everything he'd just said, all of it. "Deacon…" She didn't know how to finish. What the hell did you say after that?

But then he gritted his teeth, suddenly looking pissed. "The first time, all those years ago…I was young. *We* were young. I had plans, and you didn't fit into them. I'm sorry I hurt you. But we were just kids."

Oh, age was the issue now, timing? Neither of those things had mattered when he'd proposed to Emily a few weeks after popping her cherry. He'd run from Axle Alley so fast the only thing she'd had to remember him by were the skid marks he'd left on the road as he'd sped away.

He didn't get it, how much he'd crushed her. She didn't think he ever would. She hadn't fit his plans then, and she sure as hell didn't now. She'd been good enough for a quick fuck and some mild amusement, but when it came time to settle down, he'd chosen the complete opposite of her. In his eyes, she would never be good enough. "Deflower any more virgins lately?"

He hissed out a frustrated breath. "No, you were the only one."

"Lucky me."

He moved in, crowding her, out of patience. "Have you made your decision?"

If she had any pride at all, she'd tell him to go screw himself, but her body was more than happy with the idea of handing itself over to this man. To let him use her as he liked in exchange for keeping their garage. God, she was pathetic. "I'll do it."

He smiled and looked so much like his teenage self, her heart hurt. "Good choice."

She crossed her arms. "As soon as the three months are up, it's over, right?"

"That was the agreement."

The guy was giving her frostbite. He'd use her until he'd had his fill and then move on to the next without a backward glance. "I have one more condition."

His gaze sharpened. "Name it."

"I want you to sign the building over to Piper and Rusty."

"When you've fulfilled your end of the bargain, and proven to me this business is solid, I'll be happy to."

She had no doubt in three months the business would be more than solid. "Well…good, then."

He ran his thumb across her lower lip. "I have a condition of my own."

"What more could you want?"

He leaned in, buried his nose in her hair, and inhaled. "God, I love the way you smell." His lips brushed her skin when he spoke, and she had to fight not to turn in to him, not to seek out that amazing mouth. "Exclusivity. No one touches you but me. And I want you on the pill, no condoms."

She was struggling to breathe. "I'm already on the pill." This was so weird, talking about this stuff like a business transaction, no emotions involved—not on his part, at least. "I've never had sex without a rubber. Does that suit you?"

He dipped his head. "I'm clear as well."

She wanted to take a step back, to get some breathing room. It felt like he'd sucked every bit of oxygen from her tiny apartment.

His fingers squeezed her hips. "I have a dinner tomorrow night. You'll be coming with me."

Then his hands were everywhere, stroking her skin, gripping her hip, then moving up to run through her hair. She couldn't take much more. "Fine."

"I'll pick you up at eight."

"I'd rather meet you somewhere. I don't want Rusty or Piper seeing us together and getting the wrong idea."

He looked like he wanted to argue but fought the impulse. "You can meet me at my apartment."

There was no warning, no lead-up, he just leaned in and kissed her. His firm, warm mouth landed on hers, and she was defenseless against the onslaught. His tongue slipped between her lips and moved over hers with slow, deep licks. Her sex contracted with each caress, making her hot, wetter in an instant.

He gripped her hips and brought her up against him, grinding his erection into her. A low moan slipped past his lips. "You're so goddamn perfect, Alex." His hands moved to her ass, squeezing, and pulled her in tighter, lifting her slightly so she could feel him right where she wanted him.

He found the rip in her jeans just below her ass cheek, and the rough pads of his fingers grazed her bare skin, making her gasp. She wanted nothing more than to wrap her legs around him and grind on that massive bulge in his pants until she got herself off. It felt too good. *Deacon* felt too good.

Things were getting out of control. Yeah, she'd agreed to be his human sex toy, and despite his being a complete asshole, she was desperate to have him inside her. But that desperation was enough to give her the strength to push him back. She needed to get her feelings under control before they took this any farther, and the alcohol wasn't helping. "Whoa. Hold up."

The only light inside her place came from the street-lights shining through her windows. Deacon was mainly in shadow, but she could still see his strong profile, the square jaw, the straight nose, the way his green eyes glinted through the darkness, intent on her. "What is it?" He was breathing hard.

She put some distance between them. "Our first *date* is tomorrow. This deal doesn't start until then."

His expression darkened. "You're serious?"

"Absolutely." She crossed her arms so he wouldn't see her hands shaking.

He cursed, his chest rising and falling with each ragged breath. "You can turn it off just like that?"

"Looks that way."

He ran a hand through his mussed hair. She couldn't even remember having run her hands through it. But she obviously had. That's how out of control Deacon made her. Right then she'd never been more terrified of a single person in her entire life, and that was saying something. He was dangerous. Doing this was stupid, reckless, but what choice did she have?

That steely control dropped into place. "I guess I'll leave you alone then."

She followed him to the door. One thing had been playing on her mind, and before she could stop herself, she blurted, "And the same goes for you."

He stopped and turned to face her, brow raised.

"Exclusivity."

His expression darkened again, and he smiled. "You're more than enough for me, Alex."

She hated herself for asking but had to. "What about Blondie?"

His brows shot up. "Who?"

"The Barbie you had hanging off your arm."

He chuckled, then wrapped his fingers around the back of her neck and pulled her in close. "You mean Candice?" He shook his head. "You have nothing to worry about there."

She shrugged and tried to step back. He wouldn't let her. "I'm not worried."

"No?"

"No. I just don't like the idea of sloppy seconds. You know how it is. Why was your office door locked?" she said before she could stop herself. Damn third beer.

"Was it? I didn't realize."

She narrowed her eyes.

"I wasn't fucking her over my desk, if that's what you're asking me."

That's exactly what she was asking. There was always the wall, or the floor. The thought disappeared when he brushed his thumb across her jaw. She couldn't read the look on his face as he studied her, but it turned her insides to mush. Then he kissed her again, a light touch that still managed to make her toes curl. "Candice is an acquaintance. Her brother is a friend of mine. It wasn't a date. She just showed up, at a loose end. I've never slept with her, and I don't plan to."

She opened her mouth, then shut it again, jaw flapping like a dying fish.

He grinned. "I'll see you tomorrow, Alex."

She hated the relief that washed over her at his words. She also hated that when he left, she wished he'd come back.

Chapter Three

Getting out of bed would be a colossal mistake. Alex knew what was coming, what the day would bring, and was powerless to stop it. Kind of like being tied to the tracks in one of those old black-and-white movies and watching a freight train come barreling toward you full speed. "Helpless" was the word that came to mind. Fucking helpless.

She hadn't felt like that since her folks died, since she'd been shuttled from one foster home to the next. The funny thing was, it had been Deacon who'd made her believe she wasn't nothing, that if she vanished into thin air, someone would actually give a crap.

God, she'd needed that.

She'd had no one. No parents. No one who *cared*, except for Rusty and Piper. She'd spent all her time at her friends' house. It had been one of those weekends while she was staying with the Wests that things had changed.

Because of her situation, some of the boys had seen her

as easy prey. Deacon had found her with one of them behind the garage. He'd had her pinned to the wall. The weasel had kissed her, tried to cop a feel. One minute she'd been trying to fight him off, the next he was gone, laid out flat by a pissed-off Deacon.

After he'd scared the guy away, he'd slung an arm around her shoulders, pulled her in for a hug, and asked if she was okay. He'd been furious, had taken care of her. She'd already been half in love with him by then. But after that, she'd been toast.

Over the next few years, he'd been there for her, had looked out for her—until he went away to college. Then it was like he'd disappeared off the face of the earth. God, how she'd missed him.

Not long after that, he'd gotten himself a preppy business-school girlfriend. Emily had perky tits and a smile to match, and Alex had been forced to suffer every time he came back home, Miss Perky at his side, stuck to him like shit to a blanket.

When she'd turned eighteen and was old enough to leave the foster-care system, Jacob West had invited her to move in with them. She'd been living there a few months when Deke had come home for the summer. She'd been secretly dreading it. Watching him make out with his girlfriend hadn't been one of her favorite pastimes. But when he'd arrived, he'd been alone. He and Emily had broken up. She'd had no idea what had happened between them, and she hadn't cared. All she'd cared about was that she had him back. It'd been like old times.

She'd been so happy that summer.

Then one night, when she'd gone to grab a drink, she'd

found Deke in the kitchen. For the first time in her life, he didn't look at her like his sisters' best friend. There'd been a whole lot of heat in that intense stare and—she'd convinced herself—so much more.

The memory came rushing back unbidden.

"Shit, Alex. Do you have any idea how long I've wanted to kiss you?"

Her heart hammered behind her ribs. "You have?"

He grabbed her hips and pulled her in flush against him, brushed his thumb over her bottom lip. "I need to know what you taste like." His fingers flexed on her waist, and she could feel his erection against her stomach. "Can I?"

He'd kissed her. It'd been long and sweet and full of desperate need, and then without a word he'd taken her hand and led her to his room. Convinced that she was part of this amazing family, that Deacon loved her and when he finished college they'd get married and Piper and Rusty would be her sisters for real, she'd followed blindly.

She'd been young, naive, had stupidly thought she meant something to him.

She hadn't.

He'd taken her virginity that night, then the next day Emily had called, crying and begging him to take her back. He had. He'd run back to her, leaving Alex behind.

Jesus, it had hurt.

Deacon had asked Emily to marry him not long after that, and when Alex found out, she'd cried herself to sleep for a full month.

Idiot.

They got married in a private ceremony a month later. They saw even less of Deacon after that. It had hurt his sisters, the distance he'd put between them, and for no good reason, as far as they could see. But then after only four years of wedded bliss, he and Emily had called it quits. Not even Rusty or Piper knew why Deacon had filed for divorce, and he hadn't offered an explanation.

In the end, not even perky Emily with her college education and rich daddy had been good enough.

Now not a trace of the old Deacon remained.

Which meant it should be easy to keep her feelings for him in check. No way was she falling hopelessly in love with him all over again. Not going to happen.

"Enough." Punching her pillow, she sat up.

No matter how much she wished it, time would not stop for her, and lying around in bed just gave her time to think about the boy he'd been, about things that could only lead to pain and heartache—about the huge mistake she was making.

She dragged her butt out of bed early and, feeling nervous and cranky, got ready for work.

Holding a piece of toast between her teeth, she bent to do up her boots. Mr. Cannon's restoration job was coming in this morning, and she was anxious to get started. Plus, they had a few other smaller jobs coming in. Busy for a Tuesday, but today of all days, she was happy for the distraction.

They had three months to prove Deacon wrong. If they had several big jobs lined up, it would blow his theory that they'd set themselves up to fail, that they were playing shop.

She stood and pulled her hair back, tying it in her usual ponytail, then opened the door and stumbled back a step. "Shit." Some guy dressed in a suit and hat stood there about to knock.

He dropped his hand and smiled. "Miss Franco?"

"Who wants to know?"

"I'm Martin. Mr. West's chauffeur. He wanted me to deliver this to you." He held out a large box and one of those fancy store bags that had ribbon for handles.

"Um, just a sec." She got rid of her toast and took it from him. Martin was tall and had graying hair and a kind face. She could tell, despite spending his days carting Deacon around, he was fit and took care of himself. "What is it?"

He smiled. "I couldn't say."

"Right. Well, thanks, Martin."

The older man tipped his hat and left her with her packages. She looked over the rail to the garage below. The doors were still closed. Thank God. The last thing she wanted was for Piper or Rusty to see his car parked outside her place. She shut the door and carried them to the living room, putting the bag down and placing the box on the coffee table. She slowly circled the thing like it was stuffed full of poisonous spiders waiting to pounce.

The name on the box was written in another language, maybe French. She'd never seen it before. Then her curiosity got the better of her, and she pulled off the lid.

White tissue sat on top, and she folded it back. "Damn." A dress of the deepest red sat among more white tissue. At least she thought it was a dress. She could see the top half. It looked simple, elegant. Rubbing her hands on her cutoffs so she didn't get peanut butter on it, she lifted the fabric carefully from the box.

It had spaghetti straps and a sheer overlay. Beautiful.

She'd never owned a dress like it. In fact, she didn't own any dresses at all. She hadn't even gone to her prom. She didn't do clothes shopping, especially in the fancy stores.

She always felt out of place. She might fix cars for a living, but she was girl, and sometimes she wanted to feel like one. Sometimes she wanted to wander around those extravagant stores and try on beautiful clothes like everyone else.

Deacon knew it, too. She'd told him once, after one too many sneaky beers at Rusty's seventeenth birthday. He hadn't laughed at her confession; he'd smiled at her, eyes soft, and said, "You deserve nothing but the best, Alex."

She pushed the memory aside, doubted he even remembered now. She looked back down at the dress, and her pulse sped up, heat rushing to the surface of her skin. Jesus, she was actually looking forward to wearing it, to spending time with Deacon. Deacon, who was a controlling, blackmailing asshole.

Her phone rang and she jumped, dropping the dress back in the box. "Shoot." Yanking her phone from her back pocket, she saw Deacon's name flash across the screen.

As much as she wanted to, she didn't think ignoring him and pretending none of this was happening would make him go away.

"Do you like it?" he said as soon as she answered. She didn't miss the way his voice had deepened, sounding rougher than usual. Obviously *he* liked it.

Her traitorous body instantly fired to life at the sound of his voice, the memory of how he'd growled dirty things to her in the darkness. How she'd become putty in his hands when he'd taken control of her body, how she'd loved every second of it.

Gah! She squeezed her eyes closed. She had to stop thinking of that night.

She wasn't going to fall all over him just because he

bought her a damn dress. No way would she make this easy for him. "How did you find the time to get it? I only agreed to be your sexual plaything last night."

He was quiet for several seconds. "Don't say that, Alex. That's not what this is." He sounded pissed.

She wasn't touching that with a barge pole. "Sorry, does *escort* suit you better?"

He growled. "Alex…"

The rough sound sent an erotic tingle down her spine. "Whatever. I take it this is what you want me to parade around in for you tonight?"

"Yes. There should be shoes there as well?"

He was back to being Mr. Chill. Good. This was an arrangement, a deal — granted, a sick and twisted one — but in the end they'd both get what they wanted, nothing more. The building would be out of his hands, and she'd never have to answer to him again, and that's all that mattered.

He'd said himself he wasn't interested in a committed relationship, and she'd do well to remember it.

"Worried I'll embarrass you in front of all your stuffy suit friends?"

He sighed. "No. But cutoffs and a Metallica T-shirt won't fit the dress code. We'd be turned away at the door." He was quiet a heartbeat. "And I wanted to do something nice for you."

Jesus. If he tried to be nice, she wouldn't survive the next few months. "Well, you'll have to excuse me for questioning your motives. I've recently learned your good deeds come at a high price."

She could almost hear his teeth grinding down the line. "I'll see you at my place at seven thirty sharp."

"I'll be there."

"Yes. You will." Then the phone went dead.

Crap.

• • •

Deacon looked at his watch. His little viper should be here any minute.

He'd been off his game all day, his mind fixed on Alex. After their phone conversation this morning, he'd begun to doubt his plan. But drastic situations called for drastic measures.

She was afraid of her own feelings, afraid of what might happen if she got close to him. He'd seen the way she looked out for his sisters. The way she almost clung to them. She was afraid all the time, afraid that one day she might lose them, too.

But she hadn't been able to hide her response to him when he'd shown up at her place. He'd seen the longing in her eyes. So much so, he'd been tempted to come clean, tell her everything, tell her the way he felt, but then that fear, that wariness had rushed forward and she'd withdrawn from him, throwing up that damn wall. He knew in that moment his only option was to move forward, continue on with his plan. She wanted him as much as he wanted her, he knew this, but if he eased up, gave her an inch, told her the truth, she'd run a mile. He just had to chip away her defenses, get under her skin, prove to her that she could trust him, that he wouldn't disappear on her.

Not this time.

He'd let security at his apartment know Alex was

coming. She would be spending a lot of time with him over the next three months, and he wanted her to come and go as she pleased.

He wasn't surprised when the quiet, almost hesitant knock came. He didn't waste time answering it, afraid she'd change her mind and run before he got there.

When he opened the door and laid eyes on her, he was glad he still held the door handle. His mouth went dry and his dick hardened at the sight of her. She was wearing the dress he'd picked out. He'd had a friend of his open her shop after Alex had agreed to his conditions. As soon as he'd seen it, he'd known it was the one.

The deep red was the same shade as the petals tattooed on her upper arm and shoulder, and the dress hugged her curves in all the right places. He dropped his gaze and stifled a groan. The shoes looked sexy as hell, and slightly edgy, like the woman herself.

He'd never seen her in heels before—never seen her in a dress, for that matter. She wouldn't meet his eyes, her gaze darting everywhere but at him. He grabbed her hand and pulled her into his apartment, and when she did finally look up at him, he could see she was trying to appear unaffected. But she was biting her lower lip, something he knew she did when she was nervous.

"You look stunning."

"Um…thanks." Her gaze darted away again, widened. "Holy crap, this place is huge." Her hair hung down her back, sleek and sexy. His fingers itched to reach out and touch.

He chuckled. "Thanks. I like it."

She eyed him, and he saw that spark she got right before she put someone in their place. "It wasn't a compliment. The place is like a mausoleum."

"Do you plan on being a brat for the whole evening?"

"Haven't decided."

She was nervous and purposely trying to piss him off. What she didn't know was that he loved that feisty side of her nature, just not when she was using it to protect herself.

He ran his hands over her bare shoulders. "This is our first official date."

The pulse in her throat fluttered madly. She shrugged. "I guess."

"I don't want you to be worried about tonight. My meeting is an informal one, just drinks and some dinner with a client."

Her brow scrunched. "I'm not worried. I couldn't care less what your *client*"—she lifted her fingers, adding air quotes—"thinks of me."

He ignored her rancor and cupped the side of her face. She stilled but then licked her lips. Always a contradiction. "You know what tonight means, being our first official date?"

"That you've *officially* lost your mind and crossed over to the dark side?"

He brushed his thumb across her jaw, and she leaned in, swaying a little closer. He didn't even think she was aware she was doing it. Her body was saying the opposite of that smart mouth. She couldn't hide the way he affected her, no matter how hard she tried.

"No." He dipped his head so his mouth was half an inch from hers, close enough he could feel the way her warm breath rushed from between her parted lips. "It means I can kiss you…whenever I want."

But he didn't. He waited, needing her to close the gap, to

show him she wanted this as much as he did. Her hands went to his shoulders, fingers digging in, and she pushed. There was no real feeling behind it, so he held his ground.

Alex stood there, breath coming harder, faster.

Shit. His gut twisted.

Just when he thought it wouldn't happen and this whole plan had been the biggest mistake of his life, that Alex didn't want him and he'd have to give her up and walk away, she stopped pushing, gripped the front of his jacket, and going up on her tiptoes, tugged him closer.

Her lips collided with his, and as soon as they did, she whimpered into his mouth. *Yes.*

He kissed her like he'd been aching to for months, and she returned it just as fiercely, her tongue sliding against his in that amazing uninhibited way he would never get enough of.

He slid his hands from her waist up to her beautiful breasts, and she made a strangled sound but pushed closer. He lightly nipped her lower lip, and she kissed him back harder, thrusting her fingers into his hair, and held him there so he wouldn't stop. God, her reaction to his touch made his dick strain and his balls ache. How would he get through dinner with her right beside him?

He brushed his thumbs across the hardened peaks of her nipples and nearly came in his pants when he felt the small bar that went through the right one. He groaned and tore his mouth from hers. "Fuck, Alex. You've had your nipple pierced?"

She was still clutching his jacket and sucked on his lip before answering. "Yeah, and my belly button."

Deacon slid his arms under her ass, lifted her off the

floor, strode to the living room, and deposited her on the couch. If he took her to his room, they'd never leave the apartment. He could cancel his business dinner, but he didn't think that was the best idea. As much as he wanted her, and he did, painfully so, he knew rushing things wouldn't help his cause where Alex was concerned.

One taste before they left would have to do.

"What are you doing?" she asked, voice breathless, needy.

His answer was to drop to his knees in front of her. "One taste, Alex. Just one." She sucked in a breath when he slipped a thin strap off her shoulder and pulled down her dress to reveal one perfect pink nipple. A metallic purple bar pierced the delicate flesh, which puckered further under his heated gaze.

"Do you have any idea how hot that is?"

She lifted her chin and smirked. "I've been told once or twice."

Was she trying to piss him off? Hurt him? More than likely. The idea of another man seeing her like this, touching her, drove him insane. "Well, for the next three months you're mine, Alex. Nobody else sees you like this. Do you understand?"

He brushed his thumb over the peak again. This time without her dress covering her, and she gasped. "It's not like you've given me any other choice."

"Exactly, so don't fight it. Enjoy what I can do for you, what we can do for each other." He bent down and sucked the purple bar into his mouth. The metal was warm from her body heat, and he groaned. He swirled his tongue, sucking hard, then tugged on her tender flesh while he continued to stroke the other one through her dress.

He glanced up. "Do you like that? Do you like it when I tug the barbell in that perfect little nipple?"

"Yes," she gasped.

Her fingers were in his hair, and she fisted it almost painfully as she held him to her. She was still fighting it, fighting the way he made her feel. She squirmed, and he knew she was already wet for him. He shoved her dress higher so he could get between her legs.

Spreading her thighs, he pulled her to the edge of the couch so he had better access and rubbed his erection against her hot center. "Shit, Alex. You can feel it, can't you, feel it between your thighs, deep inside, when I suck you into my mouth?" She wrapped her legs around his waist and kept him where she wanted him.

"Yes."

"Feels good, doesn't it, baby?"

She nodded, whimpering.

Shit. He sucked harder and ground against her. He could feel her heated flesh through his trousers but resisted the urge to free his dick, shove her panties aside, and fuck her hard right then and there. He didn't want to rush this. He wanted to take his time, to savor her.

He palmed her ass and thrust against her, while he squeezed the other breast and gave the bar in his mouth another sharp tug.

She cried out, coming apart in his arms. He wanted to hear his name on her lips, but it was only a matter of time, he'd make sure of it. She yanked his hair again, holding him against her until her cries died and her body went soft and pliant.

He pulled back and looked down at her. So beautiful.

"Next time I plan on watching you when you come." It took serious self-control, but he lifted her straps back up, pulled her dress down over her thighs, and sat back on his heels. "We need to get going."

Cheeks flushed and bottom lip swollen from biting on it, she looked adorable and sexy and confused as hell. She glanced down at the front of his pants and arched a brow. "You can't go out in public like that."

He chuckled, then kissed her lush mouth one more time because he couldn't stop himself. "I have the drive to get myself under control. Maybe you can take care of it when we get back?"

Yeah, she liked that idea. It was written all over her face, even if she tried to hide it.

She shrugged. "Up to you if you want to go out with a boner like some creepy old perv."

"I'm only three years older than you."

Her red lips lifted in a cheeky grin, and his gut twisted. "Yeah? Well, you look much older."

He laughed and pulled her off the couch. "Come on, you little deviant. Let's go get this dinner over with. I'm not close to being finished with you."

Her smile slipped, and she crossed her arms.

He tugged her closer. "What is it?"

"Nothing." She pushed past him and strode to the door. "Let's get this over with."

He grabbed her hand before she walked out the door without him. He wouldn't let her put distance between them, not ever again. Tonight was only the beginning.

He just had to convince her to take a chance and love again.

Chapter Four

Oh my God, I'm a complete and utter slut. So much for making him work for it. She would have dropped her panties right there in his living room after the orgasm he'd given her. Her face heated. How would she survive this?

She was supposed to resist, be strong—instead she'd wrapped her legs around his hips and rubbed up against him like a dog in heat until she got off.

Martin was waiting for them by the Mercedes when they came down from the apartment. He stepped forward as they approached and opened the door for her, which made her feel uncomfortable. Since when did a mechanic's son, who'd spent half his life in coveralls with grease on his hands, need someone to open his damn door?

She looked at Deacon, who still had hold of her hand even though she'd tried to wrench her fingers free from his grasp several times. "Why the hell do you need a chauffeur?" She heard Martin chuckle under his breath as she climbed in. "Shit, sorry, Martin."

Martin winked and went around to take the driver's seat.

Deacon slipped an arm around her waist and slid her closer to him in the backseat. "Martin's driving us tonight so I can focus all my attention on you." His hand took hers and then rested them on his solid, warm thigh. The muscle beneath jumped and things down below started to fire up all over again. She tried to slide her hand out from under his.

"Give it up, Alex. I'm not letting you go."

Great. She needed some distance, but that obviously wasn't going to happen. And sitting here, plastered together, while his fingers lightly stroked her waist was starting to get her all hot and bothered. "So who are these old farts we're meeting tonight?" It was the unsexiest thing she could think of in that moment.

He smiled, all masculine gorgeousness. And dammit, that set off some more happy tingles down south. The guy had a killer smile, always had, and he knew how to use it. "What makes you think Jarrod's an old fart?"

"Aren't all you business types a pack of premature-aging stuffed suits?" She congratulated herself when his eyes narrowed at her.

He leaned in and brushed his lips against her ear. Did he know how much she loved when he kissed her there, how much it affected her? "You'll pay for that when we get back to my place. I can't wait to get you out of that dress."

She swallowed hard and turned to look out the window. All the witty comebacks she'd had swirling in her head went *poof,* vanished into thin air with those huskily spoken words. She squeezed her thighs together, the tingles upping their assault, and squirmed in her seat.

Deacon's soft laugh drifted over her, like he could read her mind, like he knew exactly how much she wanted him despite her attempts to convince him otherwise. Arrogant prick. She swiveled around and socked him in the arm.

"Hey." He held up both hands. "What was that for?" He rubbed at his shoulder, and his bottom lip popped out. And all she could think was that she wanted to lean in and suck on it, lick it. Dammit. If mind bleach was a thing, she'd totally wash him from her memories. Erase the day she'd ever laid eyes on Deacon West.

"Just stop acting like an ass. And FYI, you can't pull off cute, so stick your lip back in."

He reached down and squeezed her ass. "Fine, I'll stick with what I do best."

Hand finally free, she quickly crossed her arms so he couldn't get hold of it again. He shrugged and rested his big, warm hand high on her thigh instead. That was so much worse. She made a note for future reference.

When they got to the restaurant, Deacon took hold of her hand again as soon as she stepped out of the car. This time she didn't try to pull free—there was no use, and besides, the jerk would probably grab her ass as an alternative.

But that wasn't the only reason, and though she'd never admit it to him, she was nervous about meeting these bigwig business types. What could she possibly have to talk about with people like that? The only thing she knew about were cars, and she doubted the suits Deke hung with had the first clue what was under the hood of their expensive sports cars, let alone could dream of getting grease under their manicured fingernails.

The woman at the door led them to the back of the

room. The only person there was a guy about Deke's age.

"Jarrod," Deacon said and walked straight over to him. She should have guessed. He was all suited up the same. They looked like a couple of Ken dolls in their dark suits and slicked-back hair. "Good to see you."

Jarrod took his hand in a firm shake. "Glad you could make it."

Deacon slid his arm around her waist. "This is Alex."

Jarrod took her hand, lifting it to his mouth. "Lovely to meet you, Alex." He gave her a crooked grin, one she suspected got a lot of women to drop their panties, and pressed his lips to her skin. Yeah, he was a good-looking guy, but she suspected he knew it, too.

"You, too." She pulled her hand free, and his grin upped in wattage.

They took their seats, and the guys started talking. Which was pretty much how it continued for the next hour. All in all, the evening was going better than she'd thought it would. They mainly ignored her while they talked business. And since she had no clue what they were going on about, or why Deacon had bothered to bring her in the first place, she spent the time people watching and enjoying the free food and alcohol.

"So, what do you do, Alex?"

It took her a moment to realize Jarrod was talking to her. It seemed the business portion of dinner was over. *This should be good.* She plastered a smile on her face. "I'm a mechanic. Me and Deke's sisters own a garage on Axle Alley."

Deacon shifted beside her but said nothing, while Jarrod stared at her like he was waiting for the punch line. When she kept her trap shut and he realized there wasn't one coming, he shook off his stupor and served up his panty-dropping smile again. "Wow. That's an unusual occupation for a woman."

She shrugged. "I guess."

"What kind of work do you do?"

"Beside the run-of-the-mill, bread-and-butter stuff, we want to eventually specialize in classic car restoration. We've done a few already, and we've got several more big jobs lined up."

Deacon turned to her. "Do you?"

"Yeah."

Before he could ask any more questions, Jarrod cut in. "I actually have a car that needs work. Maybe I should bring it in, see what you can do?"

The conversation turned to cars, which she'd happily talk about all night, and by the time she'd finished telling Deacon's business associate what they could do for him, another hour had passed. Deacon had barely said a word in all that time.

Was he pissed at her for hijacking his dinner?

When Jarrod asked her another question, Deke dropped a hand on her shoulder and cut in. "It's getting late. I think we'll call it a night."

"Right. I hadn't realized the time." Jarrod turned back to her. "We should do this again sometime. You're so passionate about what you do. I could listen to you talk about it all night." He didn't even glance at Deke when he said it. *Oops.*

"Um, yeah. Sure."

Deacon grabbed her hand and stood abruptly. "Okay. See you next Wednesday, Jarrod." Then he strode through the restaurant, towing her behind him. Keeping up in four-

SHERILEE GRAY   49

inch heels was no easy task, not when she was used to wearing steel-toed boots.

She tugged on his hand. "Slow the hell down, or I'll fall on my ass."

He did as she asked but didn't look back at her. When they hit the street, he called Martin, asked him to pick them up, then stared silently ahead, jaw like granite.

After a few minutes the silence became unbearable. "What the hell's your problem?" she said to his steely profile, though she thought she had a good idea.

He scowled down at her. "Are you serious?"

She gave him her best what-the-hell-crawled-up-your-ass expression and crossed her arms, needing space. "Yeah, I'm serious."

He didn't take the hint and stepped closer. "You really don't know what my problem is?" His voice had gone all deep and growly.

And of course, as always when he got like this, her happy places got a whole lot happier. Which was insane and just plain wrong. She ignored her aching nipples and the pulse between her thighs and fired back, "No. But you're acting like a dick."

"I may as well not have been in the room, that's what my problem is. You were all over fucking Jarrod Prescott like cheap perfume."

She lurched back. "Me? All over Jarrod?"

His nostrils flared when she said the other man's name. "Like plastic wrap," he said through gritted teeth.

"Jesus, you're acting like I jumped in his lap and took a ride on the guy's disco stick. We were talking business, Deacon. Just like you did before me. That job could be worth a lot of money, and anyway, you had no problem ignoring me while you two talked about whatever the hell you were droning on about."

He thrust a hand in his hair—the slicked-back look was gone, and his hair fell over his forehead, the way she liked it. "We have a deal, Alex. You don't sleep with anyone but me. If you want to renege, fine, I'll call the valuers tomorrow and reschedule."

She winced inwardly. "You wouldn't."

He wrapped his fingers around her biceps. "Try me."

A red haze clouded her vision. Was he for real? "When did you become such a raging asshole? No, really, I want to know. Do you think I'm some mindless skank who'll fuck anything with an available dick? That I'm so desperate, a guy only has to talk to me, show me a tiny bit of attention, and I'll jump into bed with him?"

"Alex."

She ignored the warning in his voice and shoved at his chest. The bastard wouldn't let her go. She shoved again, struggled to get away. He grabbed her wrists, trapping them between their bodies, pulling her in even closer.

"Stop." His voice was like a whip cracking through the night, and she immediately stopped fighting. His gaze bored into her, intense, but there was a softness there as well. She wanted to keep on struggling, to get away from that look in his eyes, but he was having none of it. "That's not what I meant." He let out a harsh breath. "I let my temper get the better of me. I apologize."

He could be unreasonable and irrational at times, she knew that all too well, but this was extreme even for him. She wanted to say more. Instead she bit her lip before she said something to make it worse, which was not easy. She refused to give him a reason to sell the garage out from under them.

"Whatever." She tested his hold, and he let her wrists go but kept her plastered to his side.

"I'm sorry, Alex. I overreacted. I know I can be... possessive." He stared down at her and just like that, the softness vanished, green eyes going intense, hard. "I need to know we understand each other?"

He was back to Mr. Chill. Good. The way she preferred him. He was so much easier to dislike when he was like this. "Yeah, we understand each other just fine."

Martin chose that moment to pull up beside them, thank God, cutting off further conversation. They climbed in, and Deacon stayed quiet—silently stewing, no doubt—the entire drive. When they arrived at his building, she expected him to have Martin drive her home.

But when he climbed out, he pulled her out after him.

Was he serious? "But I thought you'd..." He shook his head in a silent warning. "You want me to come up?" Her voice quavered at the end, and she hated it.

He leaned in and pinned her to the side of the car with a dark, hungry look. "We still have a deal, yes?"

"Well, yeah."

"Then let's go."

Alex followed him into his building. He didn't wait and strode toward the elevator. Her mouth went dry, heart lodging in her throat, and the relentless pulse between her thighs turned into a bass drumbeat, so strong she ached.

Holy shit.

. . .

Deacon didn't look back. He knew Alex was following.

And right now, he couldn't look at her. He was too damned pissed off. If he looked at her now, he'd say something else he knew he'd regret later. That list seemed to be growing by the hour around her. She pushed every one of his buttons and enjoyed the hell out of every damn minute of it. She was right, of course. He was acting like a total dick, but he couldn't rein it in, not yet, not when he'd been forced to sit there while another man all but fucked her with his eyes.

The only thing he could think about was wiping Jarrod from her mind. Making her come so hard, the only man she could think about was him.

The elevator slid open, and he stepped inside and pushed the button to hold the door while Alex caught up. Her dark eyes avoided his when she walked in, and she stood an arm's length away. The doors slid shut, and he reached out and slid his hand under her hair, around the back of her neck, and pulled her in close. Her soft curves crushed against his side, and he almost groaned aloud when he felt her hard little nipples against his abs.

She planted her hands on his chest and tried to pull away, but he refused to let her go. He threaded his fingers deeper into her hair and massaged the back of her neck. Her breathing grew choppy, and her pulse fluttered madly under her golden skin. He thought he already knew the answer, fucking hoped he did, but still he asked, "Do you want me, Alex?"

She wouldn't look at him, didn't answer. She had no idea how badly he wanted to hear her say the words, how long he'd waited to hear them from her again.

He leaned in, flicked her ear with his tongue, and bit down on the delicate lobe gently. "Does the idea of my mouth on you make you wet?"

Nothing.

Oh, nothing came out of her mouth, but her body said all there was to know. Her nipples were stiff against the fabric of her dress, and he could see the way she squeezed her thighs together, the way she bit her lip. Still, her silence made him a little desperate. No, it terrified him. Made him doubt himself. Had this whole thing been a huge mistake? Had he ruined everything?

So much for taking this slow, coaxing her gently. But dammit, it was impossible when she was within touching distance. She made him insane with wanting her so bad. She made him insane, period.

He needed to hear her say it, to admit she wanted him as much as he wanted her. Even though she'd kissed him before they'd gone out, he wouldn't take this any farther until she admitted it, until he heard her say it out loud. But he also knew if he backed down, let her go now, he'd lose her forever. He had no choice but to push harder. He tightened his hold, fisted her dark hair, and tilted her face up so he could see her eyes. Alex had loved it when he'd taken control in bed, had fucking melted in his arms. She'd also loved the filthy things he'd said to her. Both things that turned him on just as much. He wasn't above playing dirty.

He held her gaze, refusing to let her hide from him, and rubbed his thumb across her bottom lip. "Does that tight little body ache to feel me moving inside you again, Alex?" She made a strangled sound in the back of her throat and bit her lip harder, but still didn't answer. He played his last card—his only option was to lay it out for her. "If the answer's no, then the deal's off. This is supposed to be mutually beneficial. I don't see the point in this if the idea of fucking me disgusts you."

Her mouth opened, just a little, and the tip of her tongue swiped across the top of his thumb as she wet her lips. His dick jerked. Jesus, he wanted to feel that mouth on him. He reached out and slammed his hand on the emergency button. The elevator jarred to a halt, and she jumped, eyes going wide. "What are you doing?"

"Answer me, Alex. I need to know."

Her gaze darted away, then back, locked onto his. "Yes."

It was there in her dark eyes. So much fucking heat he started burning up. "Yes, what?"

"Yes, I want you," she rasped.

His knees went weak with relief. Fisting the fabric of her dress, he lifted it to just below her ass. "So if I slide my fingers inside your panties right now, you'll be wet for me?" He brushed his fingers across the outside of the delicate fabric covering her and groaned. God, she was drenched, so hot.

The tips of her ears turned bright red. "Y-yes."

He tugged her panties aside and slid a finger through her cleft, grazing her clit, and she gasped. A groan broke past his lips. "Fuck, Alex."

He reached out and punched the button to get the elevator in motion again, fighting the urge to fuck her right then and there. But every step had to be played carefully, and that meant showing her this wasn't all about his need for her, that she was important to him, and that she was more than just a hole to shove his dick in.

The doors slid open, and he removed his hand from between her legs. Wrapping his fingers around hers, he led her to his apartment and unlocked the door. He steered her inside and straight to his bedroom. She looked around, her gaze landing on his bed.

"Take off your clothes."

Alex wasn't talking, but her breathing was rapid and her fingers shook as she worked the zipper down the side of the dress. She slipped off her shoes, then let the fabric pool at her feet. Which left her in only a purple lace thong. If he hadn't already known, it wouldn't be hard to guess her favorite color.

Her nipples were peaked and begging for his mouth. The small pieces of metal piercing her skin blinked under the lights, and the tiny stone in her belly button, purple as well, dangled enticingly. He shrugged out of his jacket and removed his shirt, tossing them over a chair. "Do you realize how beautiful you are?"

She looked down, hair falling forward to cover her face.

"Don't hide from me, Alex. While we're together, I don't want you to ever hide from me." He dropped to his knees in front of her and ran his hands up and down her sides, resting them on her hips. Nuzzling her warm skin, he circled her navel with the tip of his tongue, then dipped into her belly button.

Gripping the sides of her thong, he dragged the delicate lace down her thighs and sucked in a breath when he finally got a look at her. She was smooth, waxed, just like he remembered. "Step out," he rasped.

Throwing the scrap of lace aside, he ran his hands from her calves up to the curve of her thighs. "Open your legs, let me look at you. Fuck, let me taste you." She widened her stance, her hands fisted at her sides. So damn stubborn. He spread her silky folds and ran his tongue through her slit. So good. He'd ached for this for what felt like forever.

A moan broke past her lips, and she threw out a hand for support. Her fingers threaded through his hair, holding him to her. As good as this was, he wanted more. He gave her clit one last suck. "Get on the bed."

She stumbled back until her legs hit the mattress, and she sat down. He walked on his knees and tugged her ass to the edge of the bed. Reaching back, he tagged a cushion off the chair and handed it to her. "Put this under your head. I want you to watch what I'm doing."

Her eyes were unfocused, dark with need as she did as he asked. She wanted him. Relief thrummed though his veins.

Alex acted tough, like nothing could touch her, but it was all a front to protect herself—anything not to appear vulnerable. Which was why she loved when he took charge like this. She was afraid to ask for what she wanted, afraid it would expose too much. This way she didn't have to think, she could just feel.

He slipped his hands under her ass and leaned in, licking and sucking, kissing her, holding her to his mouth. Stiffening his tongue, he pushed inside, fucking her that way until she writhed beneath him, moaning his name. Her fingers tugged hard at his hair, one minute trying to pull him away, the next she would shove his face against her and grind her hips, seeking release. His little viper was still fighting it, even though he knew this was what she wanted.

He pressed his dick into the mattress in an attempt to ease the ache and couldn't stop himself from thrusting into it. He pulled back before he ended up humping the thing.

"Look at me, Alex." Her eyes fluttered open, lips parted and red from biting them. "Play with your tits for me, baby."

She didn't hesitate and squeezed her perfect breasts, pinching the dark peaks. When she tugged at the barbell there and gasped, he almost came in his pants.

Replacing his tongue with his fingers, he thrust in and out of her, so tight and slick, then sucked hard on her clit. Her thighs trembled and her moans got louder. Then she bucked and cried out, coming hard against his mouth. He removed his fingers, then sucked and licked at her until he'd wrung every last tremor from her body. When she collapsed back, panting, he dropped his head against her thigh and tried to get his shit together.

Jesus. She was going to kill him.

Chapter Five

Boneless, Alex lay in a heap on Deacon's bed. The mattress dipped, and he settled beside her, his hand coming to rest on her belly, then trailing up to her breast. He squeezed gently. "All right?"

Eyes trained on the ceiling, as if his crown molding was the most interesting thing she'd ever seen, she avoided his gaze. Her resistance was failing big-time. Deke had made her come hard enough to pass the hell out, and she already wanted him again, wanted him inside her.

"Alex?"

"Yeah. I'm good." Wet heat surrounded her nipple, followed by some teasing suction. She moaned, her hand threading through his now scruffy hair, like it had a mind of its own. He continued to tongue her piercing carefully, knowing how tender she must be.

"I need to know you enjoy what I'm doing to you."

She expected him to strip and finish what he'd started,

but he didn't seem in any hurry as he trailed his fingers down her body, cupping her between the legs. She automatically spread her thighs wider, giving him better access when he grazed lightly over her sensitive clit, then dipped inside.

He made a rough sound at the back of his throat and pressed in deeper.

"Deacon…ahh." Back arching, she bucked against his hand.

"Hmm?"

"What are you doing?" Her voice was thin, needy.

"Making you come."

He added another finger, thrusting in and out of her. She was wet, embarrassingly so. But when his thumb joined the party, pressing against her clit, she couldn't bring herself to care. "Again? Jesus." She groaned as her hips moved of their own volition, riding his hand.

Deacon loomed over her, watching her with hungry eyes. "Yes, again."

He curled his fingers so they brushed that magic spot inside every time he pumped them deep, then dragged them back out. "Ahh." She lost all control over her vocal cords as the exquisite sensations built steadily, moaning and gasping, and shit…begging for it.

"That's it, come for me. Come all over my fingers. Let me feel you squeeze them tight, sweetheart."

The endearment pierced her chest and pushed her over the edge far too quickly. Deacon watched her the whole time, never taking his eyes off her. He looked wild, panting, his sweat-slicked chest pumping hard with every ragged breath. His obvious desire for her made her come harder, longer.

When she collapsed back, he dropped down beside her

and rolled her into his side, tucking her in close. "I could watch you come all night," he whispered.

Memories swamped her of their night together six months ago. She hadn't told him she loved him, but it had been there in every touch. She hadn't had sex with him—no, after he'd made her scream his name, she'd pushed him back on the bed and made love to him. Humiliation heated her skin. Had he seen it? Was he using her feelings for him to get what he wanted? That thought hurt more than anything else.

"Talk to me," he said, raising up on an elbow and brushing her hair back so he could see her face. She noted absently that whiskers had already sprung up, darkening his strong jaw. It suited him. A lot.

"If we're going to fuck, you need to get on with it. I have to get back before Rusty and Piper wonder where I am." She was trying to draw Mr. Chill back out; instead he smiled down and brushed his lips against hers.

"We're not fucking, Alex, not tonight."

What? She could feel his giant boner against her hip, so she knew he wanted her. It's not like he could hide it. What was he playing at? Had she done something wrong? Then she got pissed at herself for giving a crap. She rubbed at the sting in her chest.

"Right." She tried to pull away, to get out of his bed, to get the hell out of there, but he held her tight against him. "I need to leave, Deacon."

"Not yet. I want to hold you for a while."

"That wasn't part of the deal."

"It is now."

She squirmed, trying to get some distance between them, but he threw a heavy thigh over hers, tangling their legs together, trapping her. It was hopeless. "You can't just change the goddamn rules."

He nuzzled her throat and ran his hands down her body and over her hip to squeeze her ass. "They're my rules. I can do whatever I like. Now shut up and let me cuddle you."

"I don't cuddle."

"You'll get used to it. I like to hold a woman after I make her come. Not that you'd know, since the last time I had you in my bed, you ran away."

She didn't want to think about that night anymore, and she didn't like the fact that he'd brought it up and thrown it in her face, either. Then a vision of Deacon snuggling with the Barbie from his office flashed through her mind. He'd said he hadn't slept with her. Was he telling the truth? Could she believe him? Had he had that woman here, in this bed?

Shit. She had to get out of here. She increased her struggle to get free, but he just held tighter.

"You're not going to win, so stop fighting me. And for God's sake, relax. Cuddling is no fun if the person you're holding feels like rigor mortis has set in."

He massaged her shoulders and nibbled behind her ear. The bastard knew she liked it when he did that, had been using it against her all night. What was he playing at? His dick was still hard as iron and pressed against her ass through his trousers, but apparently they weren't going to have sex, and now he wanted to cuddle? "What are you doing, Deacon?"

"I already told you. Now shh."

Legs still tangled with hers, he tightened his heavy arms around her, pulling her in closer. His belt buckle was hard and cool against her waist, a stark contrast to the heat of his bare chest. If this was going to be part of the deal, she had to think of a way to get out of it before it was too late. Her heart didn't care about deals and casual sex, and she couldn't afford to go there, especially not with him.

She squeezed her eyes shut and tried to control the flip-flopping in her belly. Who was she kidding? Her heart couldn't be any more involved if she ripped it from her chest and handed it to him decorated with a big red bow. He owned it, had for the last nine years.

The only way to get out of this was to buy the building from him, and they didn't have that kind of money.

She needed him to go back to cold and distant. At least then she could stay pissed and ignore how much she wanted him, how painful she knew it would be when all of this ended. Jesus, she was so far in over her head it wasn't funny.

It seemed to take forever, but his breathing finally evened out, his big body leaning heavier on hers. She waited another twenty minutes to make sure he was asleep, then started to edge out from under him.

Her phone beeped on the other side of the bedroom, where she'd dumped her purse earlier, and Deke stirred beside her. *Crap.* The girls would be wondering how her date was going. She'd told them that much, so at least she could explain the late night.

If they had any idea she was screwing around with their brother or knew about this insane deal, both women would be pissed as hell. Deacon and his sisters loved one another to bits. The last thing she wanted was to cause a rift in their relationship. Deacon and his father had parted ways when he'd decided on business school instead of the business of cars. Jacob West had wanted his son to take over one day. And he'd let his son know time and again how much the betrayal had hurt him. Eventually, Deacon gave up trying to make him understand that he wanted something different out of life. They'd never had the chance to make up before he'd died. Since then, the only family he had was his sisters.

Alex understood the pain of not getting to say good-bye firsthand. Her heart squeezed. She knew Deacon struggled with it.

Stop. She pushed the tender feelings down deep, where they belonged.

Suddenly his weight became suffocating. She needed to leave. Now. Edging out from under him, she climbed to her feet and stood motionless by the bed for a few seconds, making sure she hadn't woken him. When he didn't move, breathing still slow and even, she grabbed her dress and bag and, on silent feet, hurried to the living room. She quickly pulled on her clothes, then realized she'd forgotten her shoes. No way was she going back into that room and risking waking him. She got the feeling he wouldn't appreciate her skipping out on him again.

But this time was different, right? She'd told him she couldn't stay. So how could he get mad?

As soon as she hit the elevator, guilt swamped her, but she squashed that, too. Digging around in her purse, she found her phone and called a cab on the way down to the foyer. The doorman didn't comment on her disheveled appearance when she walked out, or the fact that she had bare feet as she moved toward him. She smiled weakly and thanked him when he opened the door for her.

"Would you like me to call a cab, miss?"

"One's on the way. Thanks, though."

He motioned behind them to one of the overstuffed

couches. "Why don't you wait in here? I'll tell you when it arrives."

The idea of standing on the street, looking like she did right then, was not an appealing prospect. "Um...sure. Thanks."

She was texting Rusty back when she heard the doorman greet someone. She glanced up. A couple walked in, both slick in their designer clothes. Their eyes landed on her, with her bare feet, mussed hair, and more than likely smudged makeup, and she inwardly cringed. The guy smirked, the corner of his mouth tipping up in a knowing way that made her skin crawl. The woman's eyes zeroed in on her ink, and a look of disgust covered her heavily made-up face.

As they passed, she heard her say, "Are they letting prostitutes in here now?" She didn't hear the guy's reply as they carried on to the elevator.

Assholes. God, she hated this, had never felt so small in her whole life. She didn't belong here among the rich and up-themselves, never would.

"Your cab's here, miss."

"Thanks." The door guy gave her a kind smile, more than likely feeling sorry for her.

She ran out, and the cab driver turned to face her when she climbed in and slammed the door. "Where to?"

"Axle Alley. Do you know West's garage?"

"Sure do."

As they drove away, she released a shaky breath. The closer they got to home, the more her panic began to subside. She had just slumped into the seat and closed her eyes when her phone started ringing. Rusty. That woman was relentless. But when she checked, it was Deacon's name flashing on the screen, and the tension returned full force. She let it ring until it stopped. *Coward.*

She slumped back, but her phone started up again moments later.

He wouldn't stop until she picked up; she knew him well enough to know that. Plastering a fake smile on her face, so he'd hear it in her voice, she answered. "Yo."

Silence.

"Um…hello?"

"You left," he growled down the line. "I woke up and you were gone."

"I told you I had to go." She was still angry and humiliated from her encounter in the foyer, and her fake happy drained right out of her.

"Where are you?"

"In a cab on my way home."

A rough exhale. "Jesus, Alex. Don't do that again. I was worried. I don't like you wandering around on your own late at night. If you need to leave, tell me and I'll drive you."

His words simultaneously pissed her off and gave her a warm fuzzy feeling in her belly. Not a lot of people had worried about her in her life. Still, she decided to ignore the warm fuzzies and go with pissed off. "For fuck's sake. You're not only acting like a sexist pig, you're being completely unreasonable. And what will your sisters think if they see you dropping me off in the middle of the night, huh? Think about it."

"I don't care what—" He cut himself off abruptly, and she heard him take several deep breaths. "Please. Just…next time you decide you have to leave, wake me first. I'll wait downstairs with you, yes?"

"I'm twenty-five years old. I've been looking after myself most of my life."

Silence, then. "Well, now you have me to do that." His voice was so low, almost gentle, and it sent a shiver across her skin, dread spiking through her belly. "Promise me, Alex."

She didn't understand what was going on here, why he was being like this, but she didn't have much choice but to agree. "Fine."

"Thank you, baby. Now go get a good night's sleep, and I'll call you tomorrow to make plans."

She hugged herself. The way he said "baby," all soft and deep, did funny things to her, things she didn't want to think about right then, or ever. "Where are we going? How should I dress?"

"I'm thinking maybe we should stay in." More with the gentle voice, but now with a hint of amusement that was sexy as hell and had her happy places tingling. "If I get my way, clothes will be optional." Then he hung up.

Shit.

Chapter Six

"They're here, Alex."

"Don't make me go, please. I promise I'll be good. You won't even know I'm here," she said, backing up several steps.

Mr. West's usually warm brown eyes looked sad when he shook his head. "They won't let you stay. I'm sorry, honey. I've tried, but they don't think it's best for you to live here with us."

She sobbed uncontrollably now. Rusty and Piper clung to her, crying as well, their grip almost painful.

"Please don't make me. I don't like it there. I don't want to—"

The door opened and a woman with blond hair and small blue eyes walked in. "That's enough now, Alex. You know you have to go back."

"Maybe she could just stay tonight," Mr. West said.

The woman shook her head. "No. That'll just make it harder in the long run." She held out her hand. "Come on now, Alex. It's time to go."

She shook her head again and spun around, panic and all kinds of other feelings swirling in her belly, making her feel sick. Without thinking, she ran, ran from the woman trying to take her away, straight through the living room. She saw the window but didn't stop, had to get away. She wasn't going back.

Alex shot up in bed, her screams dying in her throat when she realized it was just a dream. The only dream she ever had. She ran shaky hands across her face and pushed her sweat-soaked hair off her face.

Goddammit.

Sitting up, she pulled her knees to her chest. She hadn't had the dream in months, had hoped it had stopped altogether. She'd suffered night terrors after her parents died in a house fire. Another reason she hadn't lasted long with any of the foster families she got placed with. No one liked to be woken in the middle of the night by a kid screaming hysterically.

Grabbing her phone, she checked the time. *Crap.* She'd slept in. Shoving back the covers, she scrambled out of bed and stripped on her way to the bathroom. The warm water pouring over her in the shower helped to ease her stiff muscles. After she dried off, she threw on a pair of shorts and a tank, pulled on socks, and stuffed her feet in her boots. Then she grabbed an apple off the counter and clomped down the stairs to the garage.

Her phone beeped in her pocked on her way down, and she hated the flutter of anticipation when she checked to see who the text was from. Rusty.

Wake the hell up.

She shoved the phone back in her pocket and tried not to think about the amount of times she'd checked the blasted thing yesterday.

Deacon hadn't called the day after her midnight dash, like he said he would. Nor did they have their clothing-optional night in. But she had received a few quick text messages to say he was busy. She wasn't buying it, though. More like he was pissed off that she'd pulled another runner.

What if he'd decided she was too much trouble? She hadn't exactly made this easy on him. What if he'd decided to end it and found someone else to be his *date*? Someone like Candice, for example. She'd bet every cent she had, which wasn't a hell of a lot, that Candice wouldn't turn him down. She'd plant her ass in Deke's bed, in that flashy apartment, and wouldn't leave until she was prized out with a crowbar.

She shut those thoughts down quickly. That wasn't the issue here.

If he reneged, would he go ahead and put the garage up for sale right away?

When she walked into the workshop, Piper was in her office and Rusty, already in coveralls, had her head under the hood of Mr. Cannon's 1968 Dodge Charger.

She looked up, and a grin spread across her face. "Look what the cat dragged in."

"I know." Alex held up her hands. "I slept in."

"Yeah?" Concern creased her friend's brow. "Trouble sleeping?"

"Something like that."

Rusty put down her socket wrench and straightened,

rubbing the grease from her hands on the ass of her coveralls. "The dream?"

Alex shrugged, not wanting to get into it, not wanting to worry her friends, and definitely not wanting to dwell on the reason she thought she'd started having them again.

Rusty walked over and gave her a quick hug. "You think this is about your date the other night? You like this guy?"

The woman was too damn perceptive for her own good. She'd always been able to read her like a book. "Nah, it's nothing serious. You know me."

Rusty stared at her for several seconds, her intense gaze so much like her brother's in that moment it made her squirm. "Okay. If you say so. But you know I'm here if you need to vent, right?"

"Just try to stop me."

Rusty's stunning grin returned, then her eyes lifted to something over Alex's shoulder. They widened. "Holy shit."

"What?" Alex spun around in time to see a 1970 Dodge Super Bee 426 Hemi Flashback pull up in front of their garage.

Purple.

Her knees actually went weak. This was *the* car. The car of her dreams. Instead of actors or singers on her walls when she'd been growing up, she'd had a poster of this car — well, not on her walls, because she wasn't allowed, but the picture had gone to every one of her foster homes with her.

Super Bees were only in production for four years, so there weren't that many on the road. She'd never thought she'd get to see one up close. Whoever owned it had to have some serious cake.

The door opened and Jarrod Prescott stepped out, all

flashy suit and smooth good looks. His gaze landed on her, and his lips quirked up at the side, followed by a knowing wink. She slammed her unhinged jaw shut.

"You know that guy? *Sheee-it.* Is that the guy you're messing with?" Rusty hissed in her ear.

"Um…"

"Hot…the guy's not bad, either." She snorted. "No wonder you're going out with him—he drives your freakin' dream car."

Oh, God. Oh, God. Oh, God.

"Just, ah…give me a minute." She speed walked over to Jarrod before Rusty had a chance to interrogate him. But Rusty had already peeled off, heading to the office to get Piper. *Dammit.*

Jarrod slid his hands in his pockets and smiled down at her. "Alex."

"Yeah, hey. Look, I ah…I need your help. You're gonna think this is nuts, but I'm going to need you to pretend we're going out."

His brow scrunched. "Pardon?"

"I know this seems weird, and I know I'm asking a lot. But Deacon's sisters are my best friends, and they don't know me and him are…that we're seeing each other. But they know I'm seeing someone. Rusty got the wrong idea when you pulled in, so if you could just help me out, I'll owe you," she blurted in one breath.

The excuse-me-while-I-call-in-the-special-doctor expression had disappeared and been replaced by amusement. "Pretend? That we're dating?"

Jesus. Humiliation heated her from head to toe. "Um, yeah."

One of his hands came up and slid around the back of her neck, and he tugged her closer. "I find method acting makes for a more realistic performance."

The office door flew open, Rusty and Piper emerging, sights set. "They're coming."

He let go of her neck and slung his arm around her shoulders, pulling her into his side. She had no choice but to plaster a ridiculous grin on her face.

"Nice car," Rusty said when she stopped in front of them and extended her hand. "Rusty West. This is my sister, Piper." Piper took his hand as well and smiled in that sweet, open way of hers.

"Jarrod Prescott. Nice to finally meet you both. Alex's told me so much about you." He smiled down at her, then glanced back at her friends.

Alex tilted her head toward the garage. "You two have stuff to do, right? Don't let us pull you from your work."

Piper narrowed her eyes. "I'm sure we can spare a few minutes."

Crap.

"Do you have plans with our girl?" Rusty asked.

"Actually, I came to talk to Alex about doing some restoration work for me. I have a couple cars that need rebuilding, and she told me you could fit me in."

The wary looks vanished, along with their desire to interrogate Jarrod. Alex was pretty sure she could see the dollar signs flash above their heads.

Piper grinned, giving her best Vanna White impersonation, and motioned back to the workshop. "Please, step into my office."

Good God.

They all traipsed into the workshop, Jarrod keeping her plastered to his side the entire time. And if he'd had his way, she would have spent the entire meeting in his lap.

By the time they finished discussing Jarrod's cars and what he wanted done, it was close to lunchtime. As they stepped out of the small office, he took Alex's hand and tugged her close, wrapping his arm around her shoulders. He was enjoying this whole role-play thing a bit too damn much.

Rusty and Piper stayed in the office, but she could see them pretending not to look when he led her over to the Super Bee.

"Thanks for doing this, Jarrod. You helped me out of a tricky spot. And for bringing the work our way. You won't be disappointed."

"I wouldn't have brought them here if I thought otherwise." He brushed his thumb across her jaw. "And I'll play your lover anytime, though the real thing would be far more enjoyable, I can assure you. If your situation with Deacon changes, give me a call." He slipped a card from his breast pocket and slid it into her hand.

Then, before she knew what was happening, he slid his other arm around her waist and pulled her into him. She turned her head as his lips descended, and they thankfully missed their target, hitting her jaw. She jerked back. "Right, well, thanks."

"I hope you do call, Alex. I think we could have some fun together." Then he climbed into her dream car and drove off.

She shoved the card in her pocket and blew out a shaky breath as his car disappeared into traffic. "Holy crap."

As she turned to head back inside, she spotted the

silver Mercedes sitting on the other side of the parking lot. The door opened and Deacon stepped out, face hard, jaw clenched.

He was in Mr. Chill mode, and those cold eyes never left her as he strode in her direction.

Shit. She'd just ruined everything.

Chapter Seven

Jarrod fucking Prescott was a dead man.

He'd decided to give Alex a day, had stupidly thought that's what she needed after running from him in the middle of the night, again. Worried that he'd pushed too hard, too fast.

Idiot. The woman had made a complete fool of him. He'd left her alone for twenty-four hours, and she'd already found his replacement.

Alex shoved her hands in her pockets and took a step back as he strode toward her, paling before his eyes. Control a thing of the past, he gripped her upper arms when he reached her. "What. The. Fuck, Alex?" She gaped at him; her lips moved, but nothing came out. "Is this you trying to punish me?"

"What? No, I—"

"Yo, big bro." Rusty chose that moment to come flying out of the workshop. She flew at him, forcing him to let go of

Alex, and dived straight into his arms. "We didn't know you were coming." She wrapped her arms around his waist. "It feels like forever since you've come to the garage."

Try six months.

He tore his eyes from Alex, who looked like she wanted to throw up, and gazed down at his insanely beautiful, hard as nails sister. "I missed my sisters. Thought you might like some lunch?" It wasn't a lie, not totally. He hadn't seen them as much lately, and he hated it.

"Sweet. I'm starved."

"I'll take Alex with me to Tate's. She can help me carry everything." He locked eyes with her, and she scowled.

Rusty still had her arm flung around his waist, staring up at him. "Hey. You just missed meeting Alex's new man. He drives her dream car."

"Is that right? What's he like?"

"You'll have to ask Alex that," she said, so full of innuendo he wanted to punch something. "Seems nice, though, couldn't keep his hands off our girl. Almost told them to get a room when he pulled her into his lap and started making goo-goo eyes at her."

"Is that so?"

Alex shook her head and forced a laugh. "That's bullshit, Rusty, and you know it."

"Don't be coy now, girl. It's about time you got some action."

Deacon had heard more than enough. Releasing his sister, he wrapped his fingers around Alex's wrist and started toward his car. "Be back soon," he called over his shoulder.

He yanked the door open. "Get in the car."

Alex glared up at him. "Jesus. Calm the hell down and

let me explain."

She climbed in, and he strode around and got in the driver's side, started the car, and peeled out of West's. "Deal's off." The words were out of his mouth before he could stop himself; his pride had taken a hit. Not to mention the way his chest had felt like it was going to fucking explode when he saw them together. He'd already had one screwed-up relationship in his life, a relationship full of lies and hurt and infidelity. He couldn't do that again, not with Alex.

She spun to face him. "What?"

He wrenched the car to the right and pulled into the loading bay between Carter's Mufflers and Dalton's Auto Parts and Repairs before he caused an accident and turned to her. "I stopped playing these games in high school, Alex. I told you how it was. I don't share. Ever."

"But I didn't—"

"Is this about me taking your virginity? Did I hurt you that badly? Is this you trying to hurt me back?" He didn't know where the words came from, but right then he needed to know the answer. She stared at him, wide-eyed, biting her goddamn bottom lip in that way that made him want to kiss her, strip her bare. "Answer me."

"No, Goddammit. I—"

"What?" he yelled. She froze, eyes narrowing. She stared him down, fire in her gaze, as pissed off as he was. "Did you call him right after you ran out on me the other night? Did you go to him?" He sounded like a crazy person, but Alex had that effect on him. Drove him fucking insane.

"Wow. I knew you could be a dick, Deacon, but this is a whole new level even for you." She jabbed a finger at him. "I'm not seeing Jarrod. Jesus. If you must know, he came to

West's to discuss the cars we were talking about the other night…"

"He kissed you. I saw him with his filthy lips all over you. Are you denying it? Am I hallucinating?"

"Yeah, he kissed me, and yeah, he was all over me," she fired back.

Boom. He lost it. "I'll fucking kill him." He smashed his fist against the unforgiving dash so hard he thought he heard bone crunch.

"Christ, Deacon, stop it." She grabbed his wrist and held on. "We were pretending, all right? He arrived, and Rusty put two and two together and came up with fifty-seven. She knows I'm seeing someone. I had to have an excuse for being out all the time. Jarrod agreed to play along when I freaked out. End of story."

Air hissed between his teeth, partly to calm himself and partly because his hand hurt like a bitch. "Pretending?"

She scowled harder. "That's what I said. Shit."

"So there's nothing going on between you and Prescott?"

"No, there's nothing going on, you overbearing asshole."

They stared at each other, both breathing heavily. She couldn't hide it—she was as turned on as he was. That's when he lost it again. He hauled her over the seat, into his lap, and smashed his mouth down on hers, thrusting his tongue into her sweet mouth, taking back what was his. Her fingers immediately slid into his hair, fisting it, pulling hard, punishing him for the way he'd treated her. He deserved it.

But after seeing another man put his hands on her, the thought that she might actually welcome Jarrod's touch? He'd become a jealous dickhead. Shit, he'd loved her for so damn long, the thought of her wanting someone else, being with someone else, fucking cleaved him in two. Pulling back, he kissed along her jaw to the shell of her ear. "I'm sorry, baby. I'm so sorry."

Alex moaned as he undid the button of her shorts, then worked down the zipper. She spread her smooth legs wider for him, giving him better access, and he shoved his hand inside her panties. Fuck, she was wet, drenched. He pushed a finger inside her, and she whimpered against his throat, tongue darting out to taste his skin.

The windows were tinted. No one could see what was going on inside. So he allowed himself to get lost in her.

"Oh, God." She kept her head against his shoulder and gasped as he fucked her with his finger. He slid in a second, taking her deep and hard.

"Look at me, Alex." She did, lifting her face to him, and he took her mouth again in a kiss that was hot and wet. He used his thumb, pressing it against her clit, massaging until she cried out against his mouth. She was perfect and tight, spasming around his fingers, hips working against his hand. He lifted his head to watch. Beautiful. It was impossible to take his eyes off her, the way her kiss-swollen mouth opened, eyes squeezed tight. The hot sounds she made along with the aftershocks he was still wringing out of her.

When she slumped against him, eyes still closed, he did up her shorts, kissed the top of her head, and reluctantly shifted her back to her own seat. It was either that or fuck her right there in the car.

Her lashes fluttered open, and she looked over at him. "You're goddamned crazy, Deacon West."

"Crazy for you." If he didn't fuck her soon, he'd go insane.

She snorted. "Wow, that was seriously cheesy."

He sobered and inwardly winced at the way he'd behaved, his loss of control. "I really am sorry."

She glanced out the window, not meeting his eyes. "Why did you act like that? It's like you're…jealous or something?"

He forced a mirthless laugh. He had to be careful how he handled this, couldn't risk scaring her away. Maybe it was already too late after that fucked-up display, his utter lack of self-control. Deal or no deal, if Alex thought real emotions were involved on his part, she'd run a mile. Though how she could believe otherwise after that was beyond comprehension. But then, Alex didn't want to see the truth, not of his feelings and especially not her own.

"I told you. I don't like to share. Not in any aspect of my life. Plus, Jarrod is a business rival." He forced a careless shrug, trying to dial it back. Did she believe the bullshit coming out of his mouth? He fucking hoped so. If she didn't, he'd blown it.

Was that hurt in her dark brown eyes?

"That's fine with me. Glad we're on the same page. I don't like sharing, either." Then she repeated his words back to him, and he hated it. "Not in any aspect of my life."

They went to Tate's and grabbed the lunch he'd promised his sisters, then spent an hour he didn't have catching up with them. He loved every minute. Their enthusiasm over their business, their plans, was infectious. Still, he hadn't been able to take his eyes off Alex. She'd eaten a sandwich, then left them in the office and gotten back to work.

Her coveralls were tied around her waist, and the black tank she wore clung to her curves. There was grease smeared on her forearms, and her hair was pulled back, exposing her neck. She'd never looked sexier.

He didn't know how much longer he could hold off taking her, sinking inside her, owning her. But in the end, restraint was all he had, the only weapon in his arsenal. Since he couldn't say in words how he felt, he was determined to show her. Show her just how important she was to him. That he gave her pleasure because it made him happy to do so, and not because he wanted something from her in return, despite the deal they'd made.

Deep down, she knew what this was, knew he would never hurt his sisters like that. He was sure of it. The only explanation for her going along with his proposition was that she wanted him, too. For now, if she chose to believe it was only lust, he'd take it. She couldn't fool herself forever, and when she came to the realization of her true feelings for him, he'd be there to hold her down when she tried to run scared. Because she would.

After losing her parents, the only people she'd let herself get truly close to were his sisters. He saw the way Alex checked on them, worried about them. She was terrified she'd lose them one day, terrified she'd end up on her own again.

After kissing his sisters good-bye, he stopped by the car Alex was working on. "Can you come to my place tonight?"

She didn't look at him. "Are we going out?"

"For drinks, nothing too formal. I'll have something for you to wear when you get to my place."

"Right."

"I want you to stay tonight, Alex. No slinking off when I'm asleep."

"Fine. Whatever." She carried on working, and dammit,

he wanted to touch her, pull her into his arms and kiss all the stress and worry away.

He leaned in. "I want to bury my tongue inside you again. Feel you come against my mouth. Don't deny me what I want, Alex. I'll starve without another taste of you."

She sucked in a shaky breath, and he gave in to his desire to touch her, running his fingers down her arm. "See you at seven."

Then he left her, hopefully aching for him as much as he was for her.

Chapter Eight

"So, who are we meeting tonight?" Alex tried her best to sound bored but was nervous as hell. She hated walking into any situation blind, always had. She'd been forced to do that every time she was moved on to another foster home, new people, new everything. Now she actively avoided surprise situations wherever possible. In her experience, surprises sucked ass. Always.

"Some business associates. I would've rather given this one a miss, but they're persistent." He smirked. "They want money, so prepare yourself. What you're about to witness may induce nausea."

"What's it for?"

"A charity fund-raiser. There'll be an event as well, one I'll be required to attend. We go through this every year. They insist I come out for drinks, so they can convince me to part with my money. I, of course, agree." His fingers flexed around her thigh, which he hadn't let go of since they got in the car. "Though this is the first time I've donated to this particular charity."

"So who gets this money?"

A shadow moved across his face, and his jaw tightened. "This one's for heart disease research and ensuring as many health care workers as possible get the specialty training they need. Specifically, emergency care providers."

He rattled it off like he was reading from a brochure, but she saw the emotion in his face, the change in his posture. Without analyzing her actions, she placed her hand over his and gave it a squeeze. Nothing she could say would ease the pain of losing his father. Jacob West had died after suffering a massive heart attack, taking him from them suddenly and denying them a chance to say good-bye. "Good cause," she said into the silence.

"Yeah."

God, she couldn't bear to see him suffer this way. She would give anything to go back in time and give him the chance to heal the wounds between him and his old man. "So how many charities do you donate to, hotshot?"

His lips lifted on one side. "A couple."

She turned to face him. "Huh, so you're not hard and stingy after all."

He laughed, dark and low. "Oh, I'm hard…"

She slapped her hand over his mouth and shot a look to the front seat. "I'm sure Martin could go the rest of his life not knowing how *hard* you are," she said under her breath.

"I'm hard"—he grabbed her wrist when she tried to cover his mouth again—"on those that deserve it. Otherwise I'm a pushover." He arched a brow, that grin getting bigger. "You have a dirty mind, Miss Franco." And before she could pull her hand away, he placed it over the massive bulge straining the front of his very nice, very expensive trousers. "And this is what you do to me."

Goddamn. Right now he was doing things to her as well. She squeezed the ridged flesh beneath her hand, and he sucked in a breath. "You're such a perv."

He barked a laugh. "My condition is completely your fault." He pulled her hand away and held it tight in his. "Now stop trying to seduce me."

She snorted. "I'm doing no such thing. You kind of remind me of that creepy kid at high school... What was his name again? Robert? Roger? Roger Edgar. That's it. He spent all his time darting around corners, hiding the tent pole in his pants. Get some self-control, dude."

He released her hand. "Creepy? Roger freaking Edgar?"

This was fun. She was actually enjoying herself. She shrugged. "You're the one sitting there with a boner. You'll terrify your charity guys, walking in with that thing pointing at them." The look on his face was priceless, and unable to rein it in, she laughed her ass off. When she finally got herself somewhat together, she glanced over at him, and the remaining chuckles died a sudden death. The heat aimed her way should have turned her to ash.

He slipped his hand around the back of her neck and leaned in, lips brushing the shell of her ear. "You can deny it all you like, but I know you're wet right now, and if we were on our own, I'd pull the car over and fuck you with my fingers until I was covered in you. I'd make you scream my name until you were clenching helplessly around me, begging me to slide my cock inside you."

She was close to begging now. "Deacon..." she started.

"So, how was your day?" He sat back in his seat, like he hadn't just set her underwear on fire with those whispered words. "Have the restoration jobs come in?"

Shit. If he could turn it off just like that, no way was she giving him the satisfaction of knowing he'd gotten to her. She did her best to appear unaffected and smirked. "Worried? Afraid we might actually prove you wrong?"

He looked down at her, gaze so intense she shivered. "I know you don't believe this, but I don't want you to fail."

Her stomach flipped, the sincerity in his voice unmistakable. "Yeah, right," she choked out.

He chuckled. "Stubborn."

She lightly punched him on the arm. "You love it."

Those extraordinary green eyes darkened. "You're right. I do."

Her mouth went dry, and she forced a careless laugh even though the blood was pumping through her veins fast enough to make her light-headed. The car slowed, then pulled to a stop. Thank God. "Oh, look, we're here."

"So we are," he said, humor in his voice.

They climbed out, and Deacon rested his hand on the small of her back, steering her into Jaspers. She'd always wondered what it looked like inside the exclusive members-only club. The lighting was soft, and a guy played piano in the corner. The walls were dark wood, as were the tables and chairs. There were several deep red couches placed around the room, and the waitresses wore flapper-style dresses. The whole ambience was ultra-cool, totally chic and sophisticated, but somehow warm and welcoming.

"Shit," Deacon said under his breath.

"What?" She looked up at him, and her stomach dropped

at what she saw.

"I'm sorry, Alex. I didn't know they were bringing their wives."

Great.

His hand settled on her waist as he led her toward a table off to the far side. Both the men sitting there looked older than Deke; the women, she guessed, were a similar age to her. And that's where the similarities ended. They were all hair and legs and caked-on makeup. "Jesus," she said under her breath.

"Yeah," Deacon agreed. "Watch Tammy, the brunette — she can be a catty bitch."

"Awesome."

He rubbed her back. "I'll get it over with as quick as I can."

"Hey, don't worry about me. I can take care of myself." She pouted up at him. "You want me to simper and bat my lashes at you so you don't feel left out?"

He laughed softly. "Don't you dare."

The four of them turned to watch as they neared the table, and she felt like the weird goth girl at school who'd somehow gotten a date to prom with the captain of the football team.

Deacon introduced her, and after a once-over from the men and matching pinched smiles from the women, she took the seat next to Deke. They were judging her, just like she had them. But going by the way they stared at her, the way they looked like they were sucking lemons in an effort to maintain those terrifying smiles, she knew her first impression would prove accurate. They saw the ink and immediately saw her as beneath them. White trash.

Deke got straight to business beside her. He sat stiff in his chair, his voice low and clipped, and she knew he hadn't missed the looks she'd gotten. She kept her focus on him. It was either that or make small talk with the mean girls across from her.

"Alex, isn't it?" Tammy said, forcing her to look over at them.

Here we go. The cow knew damn well what her name was; Deke had only introduced her five minutes ago. Alex plastered a smile on her face, as fake as the bulging cleavage exploding from Tammy's dress. "Yup. That's me."

Tammy tilted her head and flicked her hair over her shoulder in a move she no doubt practiced in the mirror. "So, how long have you known Deacon?" There was a note of triumph in her voice, and something else, like the woman had some nasty secret and she was just dying to pull that shit out of her ass and fling it across the table at Alex.

"Since I was ten. Me and Deke go way back. You?"

The woman's eyes widened, then narrowed, lips lifting on one side in a calculated way. If Tammy's face wasn't frozen from a crapload of Botox, she'd no doubt have an I-just-won-the-motherfucking-lottery expression on her face. "Ah, I know you. You're the poor unfortunate orphan girl who hung around the Wests. Yes?" She turned to her friend. "You know, the one Emily told us about."

Emily? What did Deke's ex-wife have to do with this?

"Well. How nice of him to bring an old friend. He's a great philanthropist. Never misses a chance to expand his charity work."

Tammy's friend giggled.

Nice.

These women knew all about her, somehow knew of her past and her connection to the Wests. Alex didn't share that part of her life with anyone. They were obviously friends of Deke's ex. Why would Emily waste her breath talking about her?

They were watching her like sharks circling a dying seal, waiting for an opening to take another bite. Alex grinned—it hurt to do it, but she was pretty sure she pulled it off. "Yeah, Deke's a prince among men."

The woman's sharp blue eyes narrowed farther, obviously unhappy Alex hadn't crumpled into tears or stormed from the bar. "So…" Tammy's gaze moved over Alex's upper arm. "You like tattoos?"

Was this bitch for real? She felt Deacon stiffen beside her and rested her hand on his thigh, silently asking him to leave it. "No, my pimp held me down and made me get it. You?" Deacon made a choking sound but didn't say a word.

Tammy forced a laugh. "Oh, you're funny. And no, I don't. I've always found them to be rather common." The superiority she managed to slip into her high-pitched voice was impressive.

Alex sat back and crossed her arms under her breasts. "Body piercings?"

Tammy's eyes widened, then she and her friend laughed. "Ah…no."

Alex leaned into Deacon, who had turned in his seat and was openly listening now, tension rolling off him. "Deacon loves my nipple piercing. Don't you, baby?"

To her surprise his lips twitched, and when he looked down at her, humor danced in his eyes. He slung an arm around her shoulders, pulling her in close. "It's sexy as hell," he said, not taking his eyes off her.

Poor Tammy nearly choked on her pinot gris. "See, Tammy. You should totally get one."

Deacon actually chuckled, earning him a frosty glare. He stood then and shook hands with the men at the table, then he took hers and with a stiff nod at the ladies led her from the bar.

"Hey." He slid his hand around her waist, fingers digging into her flesh in a possessive way that felt really good. "I'm sorry about that. If I'd known Tammy would be here, I wouldn't have made you come. She's never come to these dinners before." He ran his free hand through his hair. "She's actually a friend of Emily's."

"Yeah, I got that."

He chuckled. "You handled yourself amazingly back there."

She knew how important this particular charity was and was just glad she hadn't messed things up for him. "Hey, it's not like I'll see any of them ever again, right? So no skin off my nose."

His smile slipped. "No. I guess you're right."

They climbed into the waiting car, and his hand moved up her spine and slid into her hair before he pressed a kiss to her throat. "Let's go home. I've been desperate to get you out of that dress since you put it on." He brushed his thumb over her nipple, teasing the piercing. "And all that talk back there has made me desperate for a taste of those pert little nipples. I'd like to tug on that sexy bar and make you scream out my name."

She kind of wanted that, too. "Sounds good to me."

Chapter Nine

The dress Deke had brought her to wear for drinks with Tammy the super bitch really was gorgeous, but it wasn't her. It looked a heck of a lot better crumpled on Deacon's pale gray carpet. The matching shoes were amazing, though—he had great taste in shoes—and were currently resting against his bare back.

Alex arched and gasped, then looked down her body. Deacon's dark head didn't look too shabby buried between her thighs, either.

"Ah...please." She barely recognized her own voice, all husky and needy. She also didn't beg. Ever. But it seemed Deacon's expert tongue could get her to do almost anything. She lifted her hips, seeking more, asking for it without words.

Deacon moved quick as a flash. One minute he was between her thighs, the next he was up and on his back beside her. He did an ab curl, twisted, grabbed her around the waist, and dragged her on top of him.

"Sit on my face," he growled.

Oh dear God.

Firm hands guided her higher, not giving her the option to refuse—like she ever would. She pressed her palms against the wall to steady herself, thighs resting on either side of his head. His hands went to her ass, holding her up a little, where he wanted her, and that tongue got back to work. She whimpered, desperate to grind down against his face, get herself off. But the sadist wouldn't let her.

He made a deep growling sound that vibrated through her lower belly, sucking and licking her clit until she was panting and shaking, barely hanging on.

His eyes were open, locked on her, watching, taking in every whimper, every tremor. His fingers moved between the cheeks of her ass, dipping down between her drenched folds then back. He slicked her rear, those scorching green eyes on her the whole time. Massaging the tight ring of muscle, he tested her resistance and growled again when she leaned forward, telling him that she wasn't giving him any, that she wanted it.

She shivered as delicious anticipation moved through her. Anything Deacon did to her felt good. Always.

His other hand went back to her hip, and he pulled her down on his mouth, tongue sliding inside her while he pushed that slick finger in her ass.

She cried out. "Holy shit." The added pressure, the exquisite pleasure sent her hurtling over the edge. She came hard against his mouth, hips rolling helplessly. He sucked and licked her sensitive flesh through it without mercy, his finger doing wicked things to her the whole time, until she'd slumped forward in a boneless heap.

His strong hands moved to her waist, and he gently dragged her down his body. He rolled her to her back and tucked her into his side, staring down at her, eyes blazing. "Fuck, I love the way you taste. The way you come hard for me. Those needy sounds you make. I can't get enough of it."

His gaze was intense, and it kinda freaked her out. She grinned, trying to lighten things up. "Feel free to do that whenever you like."

He chuckled darkly. "The night's not over yet." He slid to his side of the bed—not that she had a side. She didn't want a damn side. It was just where he had all his crap sitting on the bedside table—and climbed out.

There was no way to miss the massive erection tenting his black boxer briefs when he stood. She bit her lip. She wanted him inside her. Oh, it was a stupid, ridiculously bad idea to have sex with him, but she wanted to, wanted *him*. She couldn't take her eyes off his ass, or the thick slabs of muscle that bunched under the smooth skin of his back as he strode to the bathroom and shut himself in.

Nerves fluttered in her belly. He'd driven her to distraction with want over the last couple of days, made her come several times, and hadn't asked her to return the favor. She kind of wanted to get it over and done with. All this anticipation was messing with her head. It was all she could think about. The memory of their night together still made her hot and bothered. Yeah, it was a dumb idea, but she wanted another taste all the same.

He was in there awhile, then finally the door swung open and he walked out. Her eyes dropped. No more erection. His hair looked rumpled, sticking up like he'd thrust his hand in it repeatedly.

He hadn't…had he? No. Why would he go and jerk off when she was lying naked and—despite her protests—more than willing in his bed? He climbed back in, wrapped an arm around her waist, hauled her against his front, and threw a heavy thigh over hers.

Then did…nothing.

"Um…Deacon?"

"Yeah?"

"Are we going to sleep now?" Despite what he'd done to her, repeatedly, for some reason asking the man if he'd just rubbed one off in the bathroom felt a bit too—intimate.

"Uh-huh." He buried his face in her hair and inhaled, then mumbled against her shoulder. "And don't move from this bed, Alex. I mean it. If I wake up and you've run off into the night, I'm coming to get you and dragging you back."

"What if I need to pee?"

Hot breath skimmed her skin as he chuckled quietly. "Wise-ass." He tightened his arm around her waist and rested his hand on her belly. "Go to sleep, little viper."

She'd played up to the nickname she, Rusty, and Piper had been given in their teens, but she'd never liked what it implied, never liked it when people called her by it, but when Deacon said it, she kind of did.

"But aren't you…are we…"

"Sleep." His voice did that growly thing he was so good at, and she started to get all hot and bothered again. Damn him.

What was he doing? Was he trying to ease her into this whole arrangement they had going on, to be nice, sensitive to her feelings? What? Did he *respect* her? God, she didn't want that—that wasn't what this was about. She couldn't handle him treating her like she mattered.

"Stop it," he said into the silence.

"What?"

He gave her another squeeze. "Thinking. I can hear you from here."

"Yeah? What am I thinking?"

He sighed. "You want to know why I haven't fucked you yet."

Okay. The guy was a damn mind reader as well as a control freak and a major pain in the ass. "Maybe. Um, so why haven't you?"

Deacon nuzzled behind her ear, his tongue darting out to tease the skin there. "We don't need to rush this thing. And anyway I like the buildup, the anticipation."

Bullshit. But no way was she calling him on it. She wasn't sure she wanted to hear the truth. In fact, she knew she didn't. The man who'd asked her to be his sex toy and occasional date several days ago was all about instant gratification. Deacon West didn't take time to smell the roses. The journey was just another delay. Anticipation another obstacle in the way of reaching his final destination. He treated everything in his life like a business transaction, and, she'd found out recently, that included sex.

She didn't want him to *respect* her, and she sure as hell didn't want him to worry about her feelings. "Don't be nice to me. That's not what this is about."

He stilled and was quiet for so long, she thought that maybe he hadn't heard her, that he'd drifted off. But then he said, "You think I should treat you like a whore? We have a history. I care about you, whether you like it or not, whether you welcome it or not."

She bit her lip against the unwanted emotion bombarding her, had no idea how to reply.

He didn't say anything else after that, just lay there holding her. Like she mattered. Like he cared. Her stomach flipped, and not necessarily in a good way. The urge to get up and run was almost overwhelming, but she knew he'd do what he'd threatened and come after her this time. She couldn't risk it. Couldn't risk his sisters seeing them together.

Dammit. How would she get to sleep now?

Her mind turned to the garage, to the job she loved. The reason she was lying here with Deke in the first place. A couple weeks ago, Piper had put together a quote for a potential customer. A customer they wanted, badly. He still hadn't made a decision, and all three of them were on tenterhooks while they waited. The guy usually took his cars to R.I.P. Classic, the biggest car restoration business in Miami. If they managed to take that job from R.I.P.—well, it could mean big things for them. Had the potential to get West Restoration's name out there.

Which meant more work coming their way. It also meant proving Deacon wrong.

"You're still thinking," he mumbled into her hair, arm tightening around her waist. "Sleep, woman."

Dammit. Closing her eyes, she pretended to do just that. At least that way there was no chance of further conversation...

. . .

She woke curled in a tight ball, screaming.

Strong arms were wrapped around her, warm lips

pressed against her temple. "Shh, I'm here."

"Get the fuck off me!" The angry words burst from her throat, remnants from the nightmare still swimming in her head.

"Alex, calm down." Deacon's voice broke through the terror, the sadness, the pounding blood rushing though her ears. His strong arms restrained her as she fought the invisible hands trying to take her from the people she loved, his deep voice low as he whispered in an attempt to soothe and comfort.

She fought the tight feeling in the back of her throat, the sob desperate to escape, and tried to pull herself together. She didn't want his sympathy, didn't want to need him, to need anyone.

"You still have them." His voice was gentle, guarded. "I wondered."

There had been no secrets from the West family. It wasn't like she could hide it. Deacon had been living there when she started having sleepovers with Piper and Rusty. He'd woken in the night, like the rest of the house, to her screaming bloody murder.

"I hadn't been, not often anyway." *Not until you forced your way back into my life.*

"Have you tried—"

"Don't. Just leave it, okay?"

He slid his hand across her shoulder to the back of her neck. "Come here."

It felt good to be touched, better than good, and she went to him without thought, letting him comfort her despite knowing what a bad idea it was.

Going back to sleep wasn't going to happen, so she just

lay beside him and listened to his slow, steady breaths, the faint thump of his heart against her back as he curled around her.

The next thing she knew, the sun was filtering in through the window and Deacon's warm hand was coasting down her belly to her hip.

"Morning." His voice was sleep rough and sexy as hell.

She couldn't believe it; she'd actually fallen back to sleep. "Hey."

His fingers moved between her thighs, and he lifted her leg over his, opening her for him. Fingers dipping low, he started toying with her. Heating her up like no one else could.

"You're already wet for me."

Yeah. He only had to touch her, look at her, and her body ached for him. He circled her entrance, teased and tormented her until her breathing was choppy and she thrust her hips into his touch. Finally, he pushed two fingers inside her. His other arm came around, underneath her, and he massaged her breast, playing with her nipple, tugging gently. She could feel his cock digging into her ass; he rubbed up against her, hard and restless, urgent. She pushed back against him, telling him without words that she wanted him to put that impressive erection to good use, like now.

He didn't. He kept up his beautiful torture. Playing her like the weak-willed instrument she was.

It took only minutes for her to become a trembling, screaming mess, coming hard around his thick, thrusting fingers.

That magnificent cock was still pressed into her back, but he didn't roll her over and screw her into the mattress like she desperately wanted him to. He gave her a quick kiss on the neck and climbed out of bed, heading to the bathroom, where he shut himself in.

"Oh, no you don't." Alex climbed out of bed, legs still shaky from what he'd just done to her, and walked to the bathroom door. She gathered her courage and pushed it open.

Her breath stuck in her throat when she saw him. Legs braced apart, boxers shoved down just enough to free his massive erection. He worked himself. Fingers wrapped around his thick shaft, sliding up and down the hard length. Every muscle was bunched tight, abs rigid, thighs rock solid.

He hadn't seen or heard her, too focused on getting off fast. Head thrown back, eyes closed, biting his bottom lip as he thrust into his fist. She didn't have to think about it; she moved in behind him and wrapped her arms around his, covering his hand with her own. "Let me."

He stilled, then shuddered. "Alex."

Hand never leaving his cock, she moved around to face him. He looked almost panicked. God, she wanted him to lose control; she didn't want this, whatever the hell this was. Leaning in, she circled one of his flat nipples with her tongue, then nipped gently. He sucked in a rough breath.

"So far this deal has been one-sided. I've gotten the new clothes, the orgasms, and instead of letting me get you off, you've hidden in the bathroom and taken care of yourself. I want to take care of you, Deacon. Let me." She pointed at herself. "Sex slave, remember." Squeezing his cock to stop whatever he was going to say, she took over stroking him fully. "Is this better than your own hand?"

He groaned. "Yes."

"Thought so, but I think I can go one better." She dropped to her knees in front of him. The desperate need in his eyes when he looked down at her made her heart skip a beat. *It's just sex.* She kept their stares locked when she leaned in and licked the tip. Deacon bucked and reached for the wall for support.

"Yum, tasty," she purred.

"Jesus."

Then she took him into her mouth and sucked his beautiful cock as hard and deep as she could. She cupped his heavy balls, massaging, and he groaned, widening his stance to give her better access. He threaded his fingers through her hair, holding it back. His expression changed, eyes hot, control gone. He flexed his hips, pushing deeper into her mouth.

Yes!

"That's it. Let me fuck that sexy mouth. Take it. Take all of me."

This was the Deacon she wanted. This Deacon was all about getting off, about taking what he wanted. The businessman who'd blackmailed her into this whole thing in the first place. This was what it was all about. She felt the scale tip, and for the first time it was in her favor.

He wasn't gentle, but she didn't want him to be. She loved every minute of it, of watching him lose all that rigid control. She'd had enough of his noble bullshit. Whatever his reasons for treating her with kid gloves—being his sisters' best friend, or because he'd known her as a sad, screwed-up little brat—it didn't matter anymore. This was what it came down to. This was what he really wanted from her.

Cuddles and terms of endearments hadn't been part of the deal when he'd forced her into this. Those things confused a straightforward agreement.

She gripped his hips when she felt him swell in her mouth, sucked harder when he tried to pull out right before he came.

He tightened his fingers in her hair when he realized what she wanted.

Those solid thigh muscles trembled, and he moaned deep and low. "Ah, fuck, baby." Then he shot hot and hard against the back of her throat. She swallowed the load as best as she could, sucking and licking until he began to soften in her mouth. She gave him one last lick, then smiled up at him.

Head bowed, his hair hung across his forehead and his wide chest pumped in an effort to calm his beating heart. A small grin lifted one side of his mouth, and he reached down to brush light fingers across her jaw. "Thank you."

She stood but had nowhere to go with the wall at her back. "What's the point of having a sex slave if you don't utilize her talents?"

He caught her around the waist, hauled her in close, and kissed the top of her head. Then he rested his forehead against hers. "If I didn't have to get to work early, I'd be utilizing a hell of a lot more than your mouth."

Finally!

He reached around her and turned on the shower. "I just need one more taste before I leave."

Chapter Ten

Deacon stared out his office window. He'd lost it this morning, happily. Jesus, that mouth. Just when he thought he had things between him and Alex under control, she went and turned the tables on him.

The phone on his desk started ringing, and he snatched it up. "What is it, Jessica?"

"I have an Alex on the phone for you, sir. Sorry, she won't give me her last name. She said it's important."

He didn't need a mirror to know a stupid grin had spread across his face. "Put her through."

He put the phone on speaker and sat back in his chair. "This is a surprise."

"Yeah, hey. Um…sorry to hassle you at work."

Jesus, he loved the sound of her voice—it had a low, husky quality that made him hard just hearing it. But he also hadn't missed the underlying hesitation in her tone. Even though he was sure it was nothing, he found himself gripping the edge of his desk, anxiety chasing away the shot of lust like a dunk in the Arctic Ocean. "Don't apologize. You can call me anytime you want. Hearing your voice has improved an otherwise shitty day."

Alex was silent for several seconds, and he cringed. Too much? The woman was driving him insane. She was like a skittish foal—get too close and she'd dance right out of reach.

"I have to cancel our plans for tonight."

He sat forward in his seat. "No." The word left his lips before he could stop himself.

"What do you mean, 'no'?"

"I won't let you cancel, Alex. We have an agreement." Not after the small step forward he'd made with her, the way she'd come after him, taken him into her mouth, the teasing, the way she'd looked at him. His chest squeezed. He'd barely resisted telling her how he felt, those three words so close to spilling from his lips when she'd sat back, still on her knees at his feet, and smiled up at him.

No. He wouldn't let her try to put distance between them again.

"What's so important, Deke? Do you really need me to sit there with you while you drone on to some old stiff about stuff I don't understand? Really?"

He clenched his fists. "I thought we could stay in tonight. Just you and me."

Silence. "Right. So it's nothing important then?"

"Jesus." Did she really feel that way? Was spending time alone with him so god-awful?

The phone crackled, the sound muffled, and then he heard her tell someone she wouldn't be long. One of his sisters, no doubt. "Look, it's crazy busy here at the garage. I don't have time for a drawn-out discussion. How much?"

"Pardon?" he said carefully.

"This whole thing's about money, right? You want to sell our building to make more money. That's why you have me at your beck and call. So how much for a night off? I have savings. Name your price."

He cursed under his breath, struggling and failing to keep it together. "Are you purposely trying to piss me off?" Because by fuck, it was working.

"Nah, that would require a certain amount of give a shit, and I don't."

Whoa. Where the hell had that come from? "You're angry. Why?"

"Are you serious?"

This was a battle he couldn't win, not without Alex thinking he was an even bigger asshole than she already did. So he gave in. "What's so important that you need to break our plans?"

"If you must know, I'm having a girls' night out with Rusty and Piper. We made plans before you blackmailed me into being your human sex toy. I've been so busy obeying your every command, I forgot to tell you."

He blew out a frustrated breath. She was purposely being obnoxious, definitely trying to push his buttons. "Where are you going?"

"Just a couple clubs."

Like hell.

He'd seen the way they dressed to go out to the clubs. The shit they got up to together. No way was she going without him. But he'd keep that part a surprise. "Fine. Have fun."

More silence. He'd shocked her. Good.

"You know I will." Then she hung up without so much as a good-bye.

What are you playing at, my little viper?

Alex was acting differently. She'd changed the moment they'd walked out of the bathroom, after she'd sucked him off so expertly he'd had to hang onto the wall so his legs didn't give out. He'd been desperate for her, hadn't had the strength to stop it. The woman was on a mission. As if she believed that once they had sex it would prove this thing between them was nothing but physical, that there was nothing else.

He'd resisted. Just. At first he'd thought having sex right away would give her the excuse she needed to keep that distance between them, to keep that protective wall up, but she was doing a good job of that anyway.

Ultimately, he was a businessman — if something wasn't working, you changed the way you approached it. You adapted.

It was time to give Alex what she wanted.

The music blaring from his granny's mauve and lemon cottage still seemed wrong even though she'd been gone for ten years. He still expected to see her come walking out the front door and welcome him whenever he stopped by.

Deacon climbed out of his car, strode across the yard and up onto the porch. Anticipation drove him forward. He knew his sisters would be happy to see him. They hadn't spent a lot of time together lately, which was entirely his fault. But coming to the garage brought back a lot of memories — arguments, pain, and frustration. Things said in the heat of the moment that could never be taken back.

Things he'd rather forget.

He lifted his hand to knock and noticed the door had been left ajar. He'd told them repeatedly to be more careful. Piper usually was; Rusty, on the other hand, had been driving him insane with worry since she was a fearless three-year-old. The women in this cottage meant everything to him, were his whole damn world, and he'd do whatever he had to do to protect them, even from themselves.

He pushed the door open. It led straight into the small living room, and he smiled at the sight of his sisters dancing, drinks in hand, singing their tone-deaf heads off. Pair of goofs. Both were gorgeous, Piper in a more subtle way than Rusty. But since Rusty was a walking, talking canvas, with all those bright tattoos and her vibrant red hair, she didn't exactly blend in with the crowd. He'd spent a good deal of their teenage years warning his friends away from the pair of them.

"Deke!" Piper shrieked and ran at him. He caught her in his arms. "You're here." She beamed at him, and guilt over his recent absence gnawed in his stomach.

"Hey, sis." He smacked a kiss on her cheek. "Why wasn't that door shut and locked?"

She frowned. "Wasn't it?"

"Nope."

"Rusty must have left it open when she got back from getting drinks." She waved her glass in front of his face.

Tomorrow he'd call his friend Cole Black. The guy

had recently left the police force and now managed one of Deacon's businesses, West Security. The girls could argue all they wanted, but his mind was made up. He was getting a state-of-the-art security system installed.

"So what's going on here? You having a party and forget my invitation?"

Rusty joined them, slinging an arm around his waist. "It's girls' night, bro."

He looked toward the kitchen in time to see Alex strut out and had to stifle a groan.

Goddammit.

Her skirt barely covered her ass, and the scrap of fabric masquerading as a top was so thin he could see her piercing through it. That was not a girls' night outfit.

"Alex," he ground out.

Her dark, exotic, catlike eyes bored into him. "Deke. This is a surprise."

"A good one, I hope." He knew by the way she pursed those sexy lips, she didn't agree. *Yeah, well, tough shit.*

Piper wrapped her arms tighter around his neck. "Of course it is."

"I should leave you to it. If I'd known you were going out, I wouldn't have stopped by." Low blow, pulling the sympathy card, but right now he'd do whatever was necessary to make sure he went with them. The idea of other men looking at Alex dressed like that made him damn near insane.

"Come with us, Deke?" Piper said with that goofy smile still in place. By the looks of her, he'd spend most of the night watching after his tipsy sister.

"Yeah, come with us," Rusty said. "We're celebrating."

"Oh?"

Piper squeezed his arm. "Rusty scored us a massive restoration job earlier this week, and a quote I put in last week, that I was positive we wouldn't get, was accepted this morning! We beat out three other shops."

"That's fantastic, Pipe."

Alex scowled at him. He ignored her mood; of course she thought he was being insincere. She crossed her arms, forcing her perfect tits higher, and he was surprised a nipple didn't pop out the damn top. His dick filled, hard and aching. His infuriating little viper was determined to drive him to distraction.

"It's supposed to be girls' night, remember?" Alex said. "And the last time I looked, Deacon didn't qualify."

Rusty laughed. "I didn't know you had looked."

Piper screwed up her face. "Ew, that's not a mental image I want in my head."

They were only teasing her, but Alex's face drained of all color. "Cut it out. You know what I mean."

"Oh, come on, Alex. Deacon doesn't count. He's…well, he's Deacon. Consider him an honorary chick for tonight."

Deacon pretended to be offended. "If I can keep my man card, I'll provide chauffeur-driven transportation."

His sisters squealed and did the happy dance they'd been doing since they were kids.

"What do you say? You ladies ready to go?"

They grabbed their bags and filed out the door. He followed Alex out last and made sure the place was locked up tight. "I hope I didn't spoil your plans," he said under his breath.

"You know you did," she hissed back.

Jealousy reared up, cold and ugly, and he had no hope

of reining it in. His sisters climbed in the Mercedes, and he stopped Alex before she could follow. Rusty started talking to Martin, so he took advantage of the distraction and blocked the door with his body. He reached around Alex and slid his hand up under her skirt and squeezed her delectable lace-covered ass, letting all the lust and anger show hot on his face as he gave her a slow once-over and ground his hard cock into her hip. "We had a deal, Alex. This relationship, for as long as it lasts, is exclusive. You look like you're ready to spread your legs for the first loser willing to fuck you."

Alex gaped at him, hurt and anger coming off her in waves. "Back the hell off," she hissed. "You're acting like an asshole."

Goddammit. He was screwing up *badly*, allowing his insecurities to poison what he was trying to build with her. Jesus. This was Alex. *His* Alex. He should be able to tell her anything, but she wasn't ready to hear how he felt about her. So for now all he could do was focus on the physical. At least she couldn't deny the fire between them.

He slipped a finger under the delicate fabric covering her smooth flesh, pleased when he felt how wet she was. "No one touches this but me, do you understand?"

She bit her lip, eyes glazing over, even as she continued to glare at him. He knew she wanted to tell him to go to hell, could see it written all over her face. Instead she rolled her hips when he grazed lightly over her clit.

Rusty tapped him on the back, and thankfully his body was still blocking the door and Alex. "Come on, I'm getting thirsty."

He released Alex and stepped back, motioning toward the car. "After you."

She wouldn't look at him as she pushed past, and he knew he'd taken it too far, knew what an asshole he'd been, and hated that in his near desperation to break past her protective barriers, to make her accept what was between them, he'd released an insecure side of himself he detested. A side he thought he'd buried a long time ago. But it was still there, the doubt, the mistrust...the fear. Projecting those feelings on Alex was far from okay.

But he didn't know how much longer he could go on like this. Disturbingly, it was becoming far too easy to play this role with her. His possessiveness, it seemed, knew no limits.

Chapter Eleven

Alex took the shot Piper handed her and, ignoring Deacon's heated stare, downed it in one.

She was pissed, but her body didn't give a crap and clenched traitorously. Of course it didn't help that he'd had his hand down the front of her underwear a short time ago. Deacon leaned in and said something to Piper, making her laugh, and Alex sneaked another look. She hadn't seen him like this since he was in college. He'd switched out the tailored suit for a pair of worn jeans that molded to his long legs and firm ass. The black shirt he wore clung to his broad shoulders and biceps, the sleeves rolled up, showing off his amazing forearms.

Some people might think it was weird, getting all hot and bothered over forearms, but Deacon's were beautiful. All corded muscle and tanned skin.

"Tequila!" Rusty yelled, shaking her out of her haze of lust, and handed her another shot.

"This is gonna hurt in the morning." Her friend laughed, then they both downed their drinks and slammed the empties on the bar.

"Let's dance." Piper grabbed their hands and leaned into her brother. "Come dance with us?"

He shook his head. "You girls go have fun. I'll get another round of drinks."

Piper popped her bottom lip. "I don't want to leave you all on your own."

Rusty snorted. "He won't be alone for long."

Deacon grinned like the motherfucking cat that got the cream. Was that why he'd insisted on coming? To flaunt some bimbo in front of her, to pay her back for bailing on their plans? Perhaps he'd decided being with her was too much effort.

He met and held her gaze. "Never know what the night will bring."

Overbearing bastard. How dare he show up and try to ruin her night. If he wanted to play games, she could play games. Smiling wide, she made sure her silent *screw you* was there to see.

His eyes narrowed, and he took a step toward her.

Oh, no, you don't.

Before he could open his mouth, she spun on her heel and headed to the dance floor. "Let's do this!"

Oh, yeah, Deacon had been super pissed that she'd walked away from him and remained that way as she danced the next five songs nonstop so she could avoid him. She knew this because she'd cast sneaky looks his way every now and then and, as per her shitty luck, had been caught every time. His dark gaze hadn't left her once; she'd felt it, the heat of it moving over her skin. And she'd secretly loved it.

But now, instead of watching her, those green eyes were focused on a hot blonde with a killer rack and a pouty mouth.

Deacon's usual type.

"You wanna dance?" Alex turned toward the deep voice. The guy standing behind her was good-looking, tall, a little rough around the edges. Perfect one-night-stand material.

"We already are," she yelled back. He'd come in closer, moving with her to the music. His grin widened, and he pulled her in to his body, both hands landing on her hips. Before long they were dancing with the deep, sensual bass of the song.

She rested her hands on his biceps. They were firm, more lean muscle than bulk. Not like Deacon. Deke worked out a lot, and it showed. This guy was definitely nothing to sneeze at, though. She might've considered taking him home for the night if things were different. This was the kind of guy she imagined she'd end up with. This guy was from her world.

The song ended and another one started. It had a faster tempo, but she and Mr. Rough Around the Edges didn't break apart or pick up the pace.

"You got any place to be later?" he said against her ear. *Did she?*

She wasn't so sure anymore. She glanced over to where Deacon and the hottie with the rack had been earlier. She'd purposely not looked since he'd found his new friend. Just seeing him with someone else shredded her. They were gone.

She sucked in a pained breath. God, she was such an idiot.

Gripping his shoulders, she went up on her tiptoes, and her dance partner bent down close so he could hear her.

"Sorry, this was really nice, but…"

Strong hands gripped her upper arms, pulling her back and spinning her around. Deacon's furious gaze came into focus. "Let's go."

The guy she'd been dancing with stepped forward. "You all right, babe?"

Deacon turned to him, and she could see his fists clench and unclench at his sides. "Turn around and back the hell off while you still can."

Holy shit. Alex stepped between them, planting a hand on Deacon's chest. The muscles bunched hard as stone beneath her palm. She'd never seen him this angry before, this close to the edge of his control. It kind of freaked her out. It also, surprisingly—and inappropriately—turned her the hell on. "I'm fine. Thanks for the dances." She didn't hear the other guy's response because Deacon was dragging her through the bar. "Where's Rusty and Piper?"

"Dancing." He turned to her. "Don't worry, Alex, they didn't see us."

Was that bitterness in his tone?

She expected him to take her out into the street, but instead he dragged her down a corridor at the back of the club, and pulling a key out of his pocket, unlocked a door and led her inside a small office. It was dark, the only light streaming in through a frosted glass window on the other side of the room, the fluorescent sign beyond casting them in a blue wash.

"How did you get that key?"

He shut the door and pushed her against it, staring down at her, gaze fierce, blazing hot. Her breathing came faster, harder. A rush of heat, of pure lust, pumped though her veins, heady, exciting. She fisted his shirt on either side of his waist. "Deke…"

"I'm tired of playing games with you."

He ground the hard length of his erection into her, and despite the anger, the confusion, she wanted him, wanted him so bad she shook from it. "What's that supposed to mean?"

"Were you going to screw that guy? Or were you just trying to piss me off?"

Her anger flared. "I assumed since you'd already found a friend, then so could I," she threw back.

"Jealous?"

"No." *Liar.*

"I warned you. No one touches you but me."

A shiver of pleasure, of anticipation moved through her body. She tried to push him back, but they both knew her heart wasn't in it. He didn't budge.

His expression went from pissed to hard control in an instant. Mr. Chill was back, and for the first time, she didn't want that side of him in the driver's seat when he touched her. She didn't want to disconnect, didn't want him to make this easier on her. No, this time she wanted the fire, the heat, and God help her, the emotion…she wanted everything.

Then his fingers were in her hair and his thigh went between her legs, and though she recognized the hard persona, the cold businessman who demanded obedience, this was a Deacon she had yet to be introduced to. Because despite the cool exterior, his eyes blazed hot. That intense gaze told a different story all together.

This Deacon was wild—determined.

Firm, warm lips tickled the side of her neck, sucked the

delicate skin there, and he pressed his thigh more firmly between her legs. "I'm going to fuck you now, Alex."

A whimper was all the reply she could manage, and his dark chuckle told her he knew exactly how much she wanted him. That all the attitude and resistance had been for show, a way to protect herself, and right then she didn't have the strength to fight it, to pretend this wasn't what she wanted as well.

Strong fingers dug into her inner thigh, then moved higher. The sound of her panties being torn from her body came next. Cool air hit her overheated flesh, and she moaned like a B-grade porn star when he slid his fingers through the drenched folds. She moved her hips like a cock-starved nymphomaniac trying to get those fingers where she wanted them most.

Deacon made a rough sound against her throat. "You're soaked, so hungry for my cock." His fingers did another up-and-back through her slick, quivering flesh. "Desperate to feel me thrusting between these pretty lips."

She was. She was desperate to have him inside her. He kept up with the torment, his other hand massaging her aching breasts, pinching and tugging her piercing. Right then, she could easily come from that alone.

"Undo my jeans. I need inside that hot little body." His voice was low, full of hunger, barely restrained.

It was a command, demanding her acceptance, and sent another rush of heat between her thighs. She slid her hands between their bodies, and with trembling fingers, popped the button. Dragging down the zipper, she pushed his jeans and boxers low enough to free his straining hard-on.

His fingers dug into her thighs as he roughly shoved her

skirt up around her hips. "Wrap your legs around my waist."

That was all he said before he pinned her to the wall, positioned his cock, and slammed deep inside her. She gasped at the intrusion, the feeling of fullness, of being taken. She was under no illusion that this was anything more than fucking of the most down and dirty variety. And that's exactly what she wanted.

Deacon hissed when he slid out then thrust back inside her. "Is this what you wanted?"

She couldn't speak, couldn't form a coherent sentence if she tried.

"You wanted to feel my cock deep inside you? Pounding into you?" He nipped her earlobe again, sucked the tender skin there. "Answer me," he whispered harshly.

"Y-yes."

He reared back, but there was no triumph like she'd expected, just raw animal need. He took her mouth then, and they ate at each other like they were starved. Tongues thrusting in time to Deacon's thrusting hips slamming into hers.

He didn't hold back, fucking her against the wall, using his strength to shove her higher, then slamming her down on his cock with every short, deep, jarring thrust. He rode her hard, so hard it was impossible to catch her breath, giving them what they both needed. Then he placed a hand on her hip, fingers digging into her flesh, holding her immobile, and looked down between their bodies, watching as he slid in and out of her.

"Ah, shit. Fuck," he rasped. Then he seemed to snap, pinning her back against the wall. He pressed his face against her throat, his whiskered jaw rough against her skin, holding her so tightly she could do nothing but take it, take what he gave her. The only sounds in the room were Deacon's grunts and her wanton moans begging him for more.

Tightening her arms around his wide shoulders, she held on as her building orgasm reached its peak and slammed through her body, ripples of pleasure radiating from her center to the tips of her toes. She cried out, digging her nails into his back as he fucked her through it. He kept going until she felt the next one start to build. Deacon stiffened, muscles going rock solid, then he planted deep inside her, hips moving with shallow, grinding thrusts as he came, and she went over again, with him this time.

When his breathing slowed, he kissed the damp skin between her shoulder and neck, traced her jaw, and took her mouth in a slow, deep kiss that curled her toes.

He said against her mouth, "I love how hungry you are for me."

She didn't bother denying it, was done fighting him. What was the point? She wanted this, wanted whatever he could give her in the time they had left. There was no way to guard her heart, she knew that now. When the time came and he walked, it would hurt like hell, but she would get over it. She had to. Until then, she'd enjoy every damn minute. "I hope you have plenty of stamina."

He smirked and stepped aside, tugging her skirt back down. "We're going to walk out of here, and you're going to tell my sisters you're not feeling well. Then I'm taking you home, because, baby, the night has only just begun."

He scooped up her torn underwear, put them in his pocket, and placing his hand on the small of her back, led her from the office. She did as he said, didn't even think about fighting it.

Her friends were worried, disappointed that she had to go, but she forced down her guilt and convinced them to stay. Martin was going to give them a ride home when they were ready, so they could carry on having a good time.

Then Deacon took her hand, and she held his in return. No, she clung to him, like a lifeline, happy to let him lead the way. Let him lead her blindly down a path she knew was dangerous and promised nothing but pain when they reached their destination, but she would walk it all the same.

The crowd was thick and pushed in from all sides, threatening to tear them apart. She leaned in close to him. "Don't let me go." Her words came out kind of desperate, and if he'd been listening for it, gave away far more than she ever wanted him to know.

His fingers flexed around hers, and he turned to her, expression so intense, exhilaration spiked through her belly. "I don't plan to."

Chapter Twelve

Deacon woke with a start, hand automatically going to the other side of the bed, seeking Alex. The sheets were cold... the bed empty.

His stomach dropped, disappointment slamming into him from all sides.

She'd fucking run, again.

He'd thought things had changed between them last night. When they got back to his apartment, it'd been a repeat of the club—he'd taken her hard on the kitchen counter. The sound of her cries as she'd broken apart beneath him still echoed in his head, made him hard even now. He'd been mindless, so desperate for her that his hands had been shaking. This last week had driven him near insane with wanting her so badly.

Alex hadn't protested, not once. No, she'd egged him on, just as wild for him. There'd been a softness in her eyes when he'd carried her to bed that hadn't been there before.

She hadn't tensed when he'd wrapped her in his arms, she'd snuggled closer. He'd thought his little viper was finally dropping her guard, finally letting him in.

He rubbed his hands over his face. She'd run the first chance she got. And that fucking stung. But it was his own damn fault. *Idiot.*

He'd meant to bring her back to his apartment at the end of the night, spend his time worshipping her body, making slow, sweet love to her like she deserved. Instead he'd let jealousy and mistrust skew his judgment, his actions. He'd found the owner of the club, a guy he knew through a business colleague, borrowed his keys, then dragged Alex off the dance floor and fucked her against the door. Fucked her the way he'd been desperate to for years now. And she'd taken it, all of it, the full force of his need—and met it with her own.

He'd pushed too hard, too fast. Fuck, he'd ruined everything.

Shoving back the sheets, he yanked on a pair of jeans and strode to the living room. When would she stop running from him? The way she'd wrapped around him last night, he'd thought...

He stopped in his tracks, sucked in a breath. There, sitting on the small balcony off his living room was Alex. *She hasn't run. She hasn't left me.*

Wearing his black button-down, sleeves rolled up, legs bare and propped on the railing, she looked relaxed and tempting as hell. Lifting a mug to her lips, she took a sip.

He strode across the floor, trying to control his racing pulse, trying to appear calm and collected when he was anything but. He stepped through the door and joined her outside. "Any of that left for me?"

She tilted her head back and smiled at him, causing all the oxygen to leave his lungs in a rush. "Nope, sorry."

She handed him her mug, and he accepted it, taking a sip before placing it on the small table beside them. "You're up early. Trouble sleeping?"

"Drinking does that to me." There was that smile again, and he couldn't help himself. He leaned in and brushed his lips across hers. She kissed him back, like it was the most natural thing in the world, like he'd been giving her morning kisses their whole lives. He wanted that more than anything. "I didn't want to wake you, so I thought I'd check out the view."

"What do you think?"

"Not too shabby."

He took the seat beside her. "Come here, Alex." She didn't hesitate, just hopped up and climbed in his lap, curling against him. He threaded his fingers through her hair. "I'm glad you stayed."

"Yeah?" she whispered.

"Yeah." Tilting her head back, he kissed her again, slow and easy. She slid her arms around his neck, giving herself over to him, no resistance, and for once, no smart comments. Finally, he pulled back, giving her one final nip. His cock was hard as iron, but he wasn't in a hurry to do anything about it, not yet. He wanted her where she was, wanted this quiet, intimate moment to last as long as she'd allow it. "You hungry?"

"Not yet."

All the things he wanted to say swam through his mind, were on the tip of his tongue, but he kept them to himself.

She wasn't ready to hear them, not yet, despite the fact she was currently in his lap, wearing his shirt, in his apartment, without being forced to.

He had to keep things light—she was still so skittish, and if she thought he wanted more, he had no doubt she'd be out of here in a shot. "You wanna hang out today? Maybe catch a movie later?"

He felt her nod against his chest. "Sure."

His heart hammered behind his ribs. This was it, the breakthrough he'd been hoping for, and he sure as hell refused to waste a second of it. "First, though"—he pulled her ass down tight against his erection—"we're going back to bed."

Deacon shoved his hands in his pockets and looked out over the city. He should have stayed home. He wasn't getting any work done, not when all he could think about was Alex. She'd stayed with him Friday and Saturday night. They'd spent all of Saturday watching old DVDs, eating junk food, and fucking like rabbits. He hadn't been able to get enough of her.

He wanted her still.

The only reason he was at the office and not holed up in his apartment with her, was that Alex had to go to work, some urgent job Rusty had called her in for. A protest had been on the tip of his tongue when she told him she had to leave. But he knew her well enough to know that wouldn't fly.

He tried not to come in to work on the weekends, especially on Sunday. But the apartment had felt empty after she'd left. A damn mausoleum, like she said the first time she'd seen it. And there was plenty for him to do here. He had to go away for a few days, had meetings to prepare for, but he'd accomplished nothing, had been as good as useless all day.

"Screw this." He grabbed his jacket from the back of his chair and headed for the door.

The elevator dinged as he shut the door behind him, and his ex-wife walked out. Her watery blue gaze lifted and caught on his immediately.

Jesus.

Tammy had obviously had fun spreading her poison. Thank God he was in the office alone. He did not need an audience for this.

"Deacon." A shaky smile covered her face, and he had to fight not to outright growl with the rage he was suddenly feeling.

He crossed his arms over his chest. "What are you doing here? How did you find me?"

"You weren't at your apartment. I tried here next and saw your car." She took another step toward him. "Can we talk?"

"I'm not sure that's a good idea, not after your friend's performance the other night."

She had the decency to blush, but then her lips twisted and her attempt at hiding her true colors became too much for his deceitful, manipulative ex. "What do you expect when you start parading that woman around town? It's humiliating. We haven't even been divorced long."

"Nearly two years. Long enough to—"

"What if people think you left me for that trash?"

"I would watch what you say about Alex in front of me."

"Oh, really?"

Scrubbing his hands over his face, he struggled for patience. Emily had been fragile for years, undergoing regular counseling sessions. She'd been going since before they separated, sessions he was still paying for. But it was time for her to face the reality of their relationship—the fact that there wasn't one anymore, and if he had his way, there never would be, of any kind, beyond a polite nod across a crowded room. "What do you want, Emily?"

"I want you to stop seeing her, stop taking her out like she's more than a distraction, more than just a rebound." She looked a little desperate, her eyes almost pleading with him not to say what he was about to.

"She's none of those things. I care about Alex very much." He watched his ex-wife carefully, looking for signs she might fall apart. "Where's Steven? Does he know you're here?"

She looked away. He knew she hated when he mentioned the poor bastard saddled with her now. Steven had once been a friend, an associate, until Deacon came home and found his wife screwing him in their bed. He hadn't even blamed her for it. He didn't love her, and her lies had made sure he never could. But the worst part was he'd been relieved that he'd finally had a way out, stupidly thinking he could hand his troubled wife off to the next idiot. But he'd been wrong. Emily still came to him during those tenuous times, needing his reassurance. He couldn't do it anymore. It was time Stevie boy manned the hell up.

"He's playing golf," she whispered, bottom lip quivering. She blinked and a tear slid down her cheek. "You never loved me, did you? It's always been her. That filthy little nobody. Did you want her the whole time we were together?"

"No." But Alex had always been there. Hell, she'd carved a space in his heart the moment he'd met her. A scared, lonely little kid. Of course, he'd tried to make a go of things with Emily at the beginning, thinking if he worked at it hard enough, he could make a life with her. But the truth of it was, if Emily hadn't lied to him, he and Alex wouldn't have wasted so many years. He wouldn't have been forced to bribe the woman he loved into spending time with him. That was a truth his ex-wife wasn't ready to hear.

He'd let Alex go, for Emily. He'd put everything into making his marriage work in those first few months...until he'd discovered Emily had lied to him, had fooled him, had used the pain he carried from his own parents' separation against him, to get what she wanted.

She wiped a tear from her cheek. "How can you be so cruel to me?"

Of course he had to be doing this to hurt her. It would never occur to her that his relationship with Alex had sweet fuck all to do with her. "I don't know what you want me to say. You lied to me, Emily, cheated..."

"It was a mistake...I never wanted—"

"You told me you were carrying my child. How did you expect me to react when I found out you'd lied through your teeth, playing on my insecurities to get what you wanted? It wasn't some harmless white lie. Jesus." They'd gone over this so many damned times, and she still didn't get it. He was sick of living in the past, but his ex had him over an emotional barrel, bound by her secrets and lies and unable to tell a single person about any of it for fear of what she might do.

After he discovered she'd never been pregnant, he'd found sleeping pills that she'd hidden, a lot of them. She'd threatened to kill herself if he ever left—or if he told anyone what she'd done to keep him. She'd been extremely volatile, breakable, totally messed up. He'd had no choice but to stay, to get her help, to keep her secret, a secret he still kept now out of fear.

She moved in close and placed her hand on his chest. "Please, Deacon. I can't bear this... Anyone but her." She gripped his jacket and clung to him. "I still love you. We were good together...we could try again..."

"No." He gripped her hands and loosened her hold, dropping them to her sides. "I care about you, Emily. I don't want to see you hurt. But we were never good together. Our entire marriage was based on a lie."

Her eyes widened, then narrowed, and she screamed. He wasn't fast enough. Didn't grab her wrists to stop her from lashing out. Fingernails clawing at his chest, she tore open several buttons on his shirt, doing damage to his skin. He was used to this, used to her rages, her mood swings. If Emily didn't get her way, all pretense of sweet and wounded flew out the window. She clung to him, screaming and crying until he tore her off and held her immobile. "Stop this. Now," he barked at her.

She yanked her hands free, face flushed with anger. Lifting a shaky hand, she straightened her hair. "You're making a mistake."

Before he could reply, she spun on a heel and stormed toward the elevator.

He shoved a hand through his hair and watched her get in, making sure she left. For some reason she still had this warped idea about him, about their relationship. And despite what she'd just said, she didn't love him.

In the beginning, when they'd first met in college, yeah, he'd cared for her, a lot, but in the end he'd seen her true colors. At times she could be incredibly cruel and selfish, and because of that his feelings toward her had changed.

He'd broken it off and felt nothing but relief.

Then he'd gone home, and in the space of a year Alex had blossomed. He hadn't been blind; she'd always been attractive and it wasn't a surprise she was a knockout, but there'd been something else, a boost in confidence, a peacefulness that hadn't been there before. Leaving the foster system had changed the once scared, insecure girl. Yeah, those things had still been there, but a weight had been lifted from her narrow shoulders, and it had shone through, lighting her up like a ray of sunshine.

When she'd walked into the kitchen late one night, wearing of all things, one of his old T-shirts, he'd felt blindsided. He'd realized he wanted her, wanted a taste of her so badly he would have happily gotten down on his knees and begged.

But she'd come to him without reservation. She'd let him kiss her. God, that kiss. Her heart had been hammering faster than his. The sweet, inexperienced way she'd kissed him back had turned him inside out. He hadn't planned on taking her virginity that night. Sex wasn't what he'd intended when he led her to his room. He'd just wanted her in his bed for a few hours, wanted to make out some more, talk to her. It'd been months since he'd really talked to her, he'd been so busy with school, and Emily.

But then they'd kissed some more, and Alex had shimmied out of his shirt and wrapped her legs around his hips. In that moment he'd been gone, completely lost to her.

And then, then she'd whispered, "Please."

The longing in that one word, the need, it had lit him up like a lightbulb switching on. He'd known in that moment Alex was it for him.

The memory was so vivid it could have happened yesterday. The way she'd trembled in his arms, her soft cry as he'd pushed inside her for the first time, the way she'd begged him not to stop when he'd tried to pull away, worried that he'd hurt her. The single tear that had slid down her cheek after she'd come apart beneath him.

He couldn't mess this up, not again. And he sure as hell couldn't let Emily stand in his way anymore. Steve needed to take control of the situation. It was time to cut the ties and move on; they'd been stuck in this destructive cycle long enough.

The last thing he wanted to do right now was go away for two days. Now that he had Alex where he wanted her again, he could barely handle a few hours away from her. He cursed when he looked down and took in the condition of his shirt. Makeup stained the front and collar.

He only had the remainder of the day left before he had to leave for his trip, and he planned on spending it with Alex. And as much as he wanted to spend those hours in bed, this was the perfect opportunity to show her she was so much more than a convenient fuck. Plus, if he got her into bed now, he wouldn't be able to leave.

Doing up his jacket to hide his shirt, he grabbed his briefcase and headed down to the parking garage. Time for home, a quick change of clothes, then he was taking Alex out. He wanted to treat her, make her feel special.

She was in for an afternoon of shopping.

Chapter Thirteen

"Can you believe that asshole?" Rusty planted her hands on her hips. "He looked me right in the eye and said, 'Women should be home having babies, not fixin' cars,' then turned his sexist ass around and walked out." She threw her hands up. "Who says shit like that?"

Alex curled her lip in disgust but did her best to calm her friend rather than fuel the fire. Rusty had a temper, and this asshole had hit every one of her hot buttons. "The guy's a dick. He's not the first and he won't be the last who'll think crap like that. At this point all we can do is work our asses off and prove them all wrong."

Her friend's spine lost some of its steel. "I know you're right, but it still pisses me the hell off." They walked out of the garage, and Rusty locked up. "You got plans for the rest of the day?"

They didn't usually work Sunday, but an urgent job had come up, which meant they could charge at a higher rate.

Not something they could turn down right now. "I plan on chilling on the couch and pretending to watch TV but really napping."

Rusty grinned. "Hard weekend, huh?"

She inwardly winced. "Yeah, something like that." She'd only left Deacon because the job had come up. She'd probably still be with him right now if it hadn't.

Rusty snorted. "You've turned into such a prude."

"Have not." It was just easier saying nothing than lying to her friends constantly.

"Have too."

"Have not."

"Have too."

"Jesus!" Alex crossed her arms. "Fine. You've got me. I'm a prude."

"I know. That's what I just said."

"You're a pain in the ass, you know that, right?"

"It's my one true goal in life." Rusty tilted her head toward the cottage. "Okay, Mary Poppins, me and Pipe plan on having a big night at the grocery store. You sure you don't want to blow off your nap and party it up at Costco with us?"

"Tempting, but I'll pass."

"Spoilsport." Rusty slapped her ass, then headed off across the parking lot toward the cottage, calling over her shoulder, "Catch you tomorrow."

Alex watched her friend go and shook her head. The woman was a nut. She climbed the stairs to her place, then headed straight for the shower.

She'd just finished drying off and wrapped her towel around her chest when someone knocked on the door.

"Hang on!" She kicked the clothes she'd stripped off out of the way, jogged to the door, and opened up.

Deacon stood there, a smile on his face, then his gaze dropped and his sexy grin slipped. "Christ." His gaze flew to hers, and he was scowling.

"What? I wasn't expecting company." She held the door wide. "You wanna wait while I get dressed?"

"No," he growled.

"No?" The way he said it had her body heating, desperate for the guy in a split second. Not that it had really cooled completely after spending most of the weekend together.

He shook his head and stepped inside her place, forcing her to back up. "I came here with good intentions. I'd decided to take you shopping. I hadn't planned on fucking you." He slid his fingers around the back of her neck and fisted her damp hair. "If I take you to bed, I won't want to leave. I'll miss my flight and a very important meeting." He leaned in, nipped her lower lip, his hungry gaze moving over her bare shoulders, the tops of her breasts. "Answering your door like this, you've messed up all my plans."

"It's a dilemma, all right." Deacon had told her the day before that he was going away, but suddenly the idea of not seeing him for forty-eight hours straight didn't hold the appeal she thought it would. "So what are you going to do about it?" She tugged on the towel and let it fall at her feet.

He sucked in a breath. "Since you're forcing my hand, it looks like I have no choice." He spun her around, hands going to her hips, pulling her into him, and rubbed the hard ridge of his erection against her bare ass. She moaned softly, couldn't help it, a tremor moving through her body as soon as he took control. God, she loved it.

"I still plan on taking you shopping," he rasped against her ear. "I want to see you try on beautiful dresses in all the best stores, baby. Do you remember when you told me that?" he chuckled. "You were seventeen and buzzed on the beer you and my sisters stole from the old man."

Her belly did a happy flutter. She twisted, looking at him over her shoulder. "You remember?"

"Of course. I wanted to be the one to do that for you so badly, to make your secret wish come true." He brushed his lips against her throat. "Now I can. But for me to give you that, our only option at this point is hard and fast." He walked her forward until they stood in front of her tiny kitchen table. "Bend over, Alex. Hold the edge tight."

She shivered at the rasp of his voice, his warm breath against her neck, and did as he asked.

"Very good." He slid his hand from the base of her neck down her spine and over her ass, then dipped down between her cheeks. One of his fingers slid the length of her slit, grazing her throbbing clit. "You wet for me?"

"Yes," she whispered. All he had to do was touch her.

He groaned and slid his finger deep inside, holding it there and swirling the digit. He trailed hot kisses up her side and over her shoulder, then bit gently on her earlobe. "You ready for me?"

She arched back, lifting her ass higher, needing more. "God, yes."

The soft *clink* of his belt buckle being undone followed by his zipper coming down made her shiver. The fact that she was completely naked and he was still fully clothed was a massive turn-on. "Spread your legs wider, let me see how much you want it."

She stepped out, doing as he asked.

His hand went back to her ass, skimming her heated skin, then he squeezed. "You're a very bad girl for tempting me like this. Maybe I'll punish you, what do you think?" His voice was rough, but there was also a teasing, playful note that she loved.

She sucked in a breath, excitement thrumming through her now trembling body. "What do you have in mind?"

"I think you need a spanking for answering the door in nothing but a towel, for making my cock so hard when I had plans for us, for making me lose control."

The ache between her legs was relentless, and she tried to squeeze them together, but Deke's hands went to her thighs, fingers digging in, stopping her.

"Have you ever been spanked before, baby?"

She shook her head. "No." Her voice sounded ragged, hungry.

The hand on her ass disappeared, then came down sharply. She cried out, but not in pain, not really. He hadn't hit her hard, just enough for a slight sting. He smoothed his palm over the point of contact, and the sting vanished quickly, leaving a dull ache that seemed to be connected directly to her clit. She whimpered and lifted her ass higher.

Deke chuckled. "Like that, do you?"

"Yes."

The air in the room changed instantly, became electric. "Does my dirty girl want another one?"

"Yes. Please."

"Fuck, baby." All playfulness had left his voice. Then he did it again. And again, until she was so turned on her thighs were slick and she was panting, hanging onto the table like a lifeline.

"I need you," she rasped.

His hand vanished, and a second later she felt the hot head of his cock brushing her ass cheek, sliding down the cleft. "Gonna fuck you so hard, you'll still feel me while I'm gone. You won't forget who this beautiful body belongs to."

Her inner muscles contracted at the rough, needy sound of his voice. His words should piss her off, but instead they turned her on more. She didn't know what that said about her, and right then she didn't care. If she didn't have him inside her soon, she'd dissolve into a desperate puddle at his feet. "God, Deke, do me already."

He laughed, the sound dark and full of sensual promise. She felt another rush of liquid heat slick her thighs, and she knew he saw it when the laugh broke off into a groan and he cursed under his breath.

"Shit. Hold on." Wrapping his arm around her hips, he slid the head of his cock through her folds, then slammed up inside her.

"Ahh." She gripped the edge of the table, pushing back.

"So fucking perfect," he rasped, planted deep, grinding against her ass. "You're so tight. You were made to take my cock, Alex, only mine."

His rough words were crude and arrogant as hell, but they did things to her, really good things. She loved all the deliciously dirty stuff that came out of his mouth when he was turned on, buried inside her. Loved how the polish, the controlled businessman dissolved when he had her pinned beneath him.

He slid out almost completely, then thrust back into her, tilting his hips so he hit her just right every damn time. She barely kept her footing, high on her toes, and had to use the strength in her arms to push back, absorbing every brutal thrust. He pounded into her, his deep grunts of pleasure, the wet, arousing sound of his cock moving in and out of her ringing in her ears. She arched her back, circled her hips, and he hissed out a sharp breath.

"Can you feel how deep I am?" he gritted out. "All mine."

He changed rhythm, his thrusts deep and slow, and she whimpered, so close. "Deacon…please."

His fisted her hair, still buried deep inside, and forced her to turn her head. "Say it."

She knew what he wanted to hear. She also knew what saying it would cost her. But right then she was powerless to fight his hold over her. "Y-yes. I'm yours."

He made a sound between a growl and groan, then withdrew and slammed back in. Her inner walls quivered, right on the edge. "That's right. And no one touches what's mine, do they, Alex?"

"No," she gasped.

He released her hair and gripped her hips, increasing the speed of his thrusts. God, still so deep. She knew he was right—she would feel him for days, and she loved that idea, wanted to feel him every time she moved, every time she sat down. One of his hands came around, cupping her between the legs, teasing her clit. He pressed down firmly, then circled her slowly.

His other hand slid under her, over her belly, up to her ribs, then lifted her so her back was flush against his chest. The small buttons of his shirt pressed into her bare skin, making the whole thing hotter somehow. He reached up and cupped her breast, massaging her oversensitive flesh. "Come for me, Alex. I want to feel you squeeze my cock nice and tight."

At those needy words rasped against her ear, she had no choice but to obey, crying out his name as wave after wave of intense pleasure slammed through her. Deacon's thrusts became erratic, then he planted himself and came, shot after shot hitting her deep, setting off tiny aftershocks. He groaned against her hair, his body shaking behind her.

If he hadn't been holding her upright, she would have fallen on her ass.

He placed a finger under her chin and tilted her head to the side so he could see her face. "All right?"

He slid from her body, and she nodded, turned in his arms so she could rest her hands on his chest. "Well, I think you got what you wanted. I'll be feeling you for days."

Those warm hands slid down her back to cup her butt and squeezed. "Good. My work here is done."

"You're such a Neanderthal."

He shrugged. "I've told you before, I don't share. I wanted to leave you with a reminder."

She tensed. Okay, that stung. She'd promised not to sleep with anyone else, but it was obvious he didn't trust her. This wasn't the first time he'd said something like that, accused her of looking elsewhere. She pulled away and tried to back up, but he grabbed her upper arms and held her where he wanted her.

"Whoa, what's going on?" He frowned, looking genuinely confused. "Why are you pulling away?"

She crossed her arms. "You're obviously used to sleeping with lying bimbos. So I'm gonna spell it out for you. When I make a promise, I keep it. I said I wouldn't sleep with anyone else during our arrangement, and I meant it. You need to stop with the accusations."

He dragged her up against him. "I know that. I do."

"You sure about that? Cause I'm kinda getting the impression you think I'll jump on the first dick that pops up in front of me."

He tucked her hair behind her ear. "I'm sorry. I know that's not you. I just hate that I have to go away. I'm taking my crappy mood out on you."

She wasn't buying it—there was more to it, a hell of a lot more, but she decided to leave it alone. He was going away, and she didn't want to argue before he left. So instead she smiled up at him. "How can you be pissed after that?" She tilted her head toward the table, and he chuckled.

"Because now I want more of you and I know I can't have you. Not till I get back." The sincerity in his gaze made her chest tight. She could see more than just lust, there was warmth and affection there as well. *Don't read more into it.*

They had a long history. The look in his eyes said nothing more than that, meant nothing more than a shared past with his kid sisters' best friend. And that's how she wanted it, right? Fuck buddies. She could do that. She'd been momentarily thrown off course, had let those old feelings, the sad kid with the stupid crush, rear their head. This was nothing. It was fun, a mutually beneficial agreement and nothing more.

Deacon had made his feelings about commitment and relationships clear, and she didn't want more than that from him, didn't want more than that from anyone. Suddenly she felt lighter than she had all week. She didn't need to get all twisted up in knots about this. It was simple. Fun.

She grinned up at him. "How about I cook you dinner when you get back? Would that improve your mood?"

He smiled wide, flashing white teeth and his elusive dimple that only made an appearance when he was really happy. "I'd love that."

She gripped the side of his neck, needing to touch bare skin. The action was unconscious, a result of letting go of all the angst, all the *what if*s, and embracing the moment. Taking pleasure from one another without all the messy feelings. "You up for a little cloak and dagger?"

"What do you have in mind?"

"Maybe you could borrow Martin's car or something? That way your sisters won't get suspicious and I get to cook in my own kitchen, tiny and crappy as it is. You okay with that?"

His hands slid down her waist, back to her butt. "More than okay."

"Awesome." She knew she had a goofy-assed grin on her face but didn't care.

He gave her butt cheek a light squeeze, and she bit her lip, still deliciously sensitive. "Now go get dressed." His voice dipped lower. "I want to take you shopping. The real reason I came here in the first place, before you seduced me."

"Mmm-hmm, just keep telling yourself that if it makes you feel better." She patted his chest. "I know the truth."

"Oh, yeah, what's that?"

"You're a dirty old perv."

She danced out of reach when he tried to grab her, and his low chuckle followed her into her bedroom. "I'll make you pay for that when I get back, you know that, right?"

Oh, she was counting on it, and she couldn't wait.

Chapter Fourteen

"I told you to stop looking at the price tags." Deacon frowned and pulled the dress out of Alex's hands, then passed it to the shop assistant hovering behind them. "Take this to the changing room as well, please."

His little viper crossed her arms and threw him a pissy look. He didn't dare tell her she looked cute and sexy all riled up. "No one can see the labels when I'm wearing them." She leaned in, lowering her voice. "So why are you insisting we shop where a single dress costs more than… than…shit, I can't think of anything to compare it to. What does that tell you?"

"That you're not very imaginative?"

She released a drawn-out sigh that made his dick stand up and take notice. But then, all the woman had to do was look at him and his dick took notice. "No, wise-ass, it tells you that you're wasting your money. I work in a filthy garage, elbows deep in grease every day. Getting me stuff like this is a waste."

He quirked a brow. "Can you repeat that please?"

She crossed her arms and scowled.

"You know, the part after you called me a wise-ass."

She rolled her eyes.

"The part where you said I'm wasting *my* money."

"God, you're annoying."

"I know. Now stop acting like a brat and get in the changing room and try on those extremely beautiful, obscenely expensive dresses and pretend you're enjoying yourself."

A grin lifted the corner of her mouth, just a bit, but enough. "It's that important to you?"

He'd seen the way her eyes had lit up when they'd walked in the door. The designer clothes were more on the edgy side, unique, like the woman standing in front of him, and he'd hoped more her style than the places he'd been shopping for her so far.

Alex could deny it all she wanted, but he knew she was full of it. "Yes. It's that important to me."

"Fine." Lifting the small leather bag she'd strung across her shoulder over her head, she thrust it at him. "Here, hold my purse." He didn't miss the wicked glint in her eyes as she all but stomped to the dressing room.

Oh, yeah, she'll pay for that, too.

He'd had her bent over her kitchen table less than two hours ago, and he could hardly wait to have her in his bed again, to take his time, to savor every minute. The last few times had been hard and fast—his desperation to quench his need for her hadn't allowed anything else—but he intended to show her how good it could be when he took his time... when he made love to her.

He grinned. And he'd do just that, as soon as he got back.

He glanced over to the changing rooms and shook his head. Despite her protests, she was enjoying herself. The afternoon couldn't be going better. He'd taken her to lunch first, and they'd talked the whole time, laughed, and when they'd left, she'd let him take her hand, had actually kissed him as a thank-you. The first kiss she'd initiated, for no other reason than she'd wanted to. It was perfect and had driven him damn near crazy, especially when she'd slid her tongue along his bottom lip before pulling away.

His blood fired at the memory, but he reined it in. Today wasn't about satisfying his lust for her. He wanted to show her how good they were together, and not just in bed.

He moved to the far wall, where the shoes were displayed, and waved the assistant over. "I'll take these boots as well. Size seven." Alex had picked them up and all but drooled over them, but after checking the price had shoved them back like they were on fire. He'd seen her cast longing looks their way several times since. The black boots were knee-high and had a row of silver studs around the top of each spiked heel. They were extremely sexy, sleek, edgy. They were made for Alex.

He wanted to see her in these sexy, kick-ass boots, and nothing else. Talk about torturing himself.

"Silver studs, Deacon? I didn't think they were your style."

He turned at the sound of his ex-wife's voice, taking in her appearance. There was no trace of the emotional breakdown from his office that morning. She was perfectly put together, not a hair out of place. Tammy stood beside her, a vicious smile lifting her glossy red lips. "I'm surprised to see you out and about, Emily. I take it you're feeling better?"

She straightened her shoulders. "Don't tell me you're concerned." She looked at her friend, then back to him. "And how is it any of your business?"

"It's not, you're absolutely right." He turned his back on them and headed to the dressing rooms just as Alex stepped out in the purple satin slip dress she'd spotted as soon as they'd walked in. *Shit.* She looked amazing. The woman stole his breath.

Her nose crinkled in a cute way that made him want to pull her into his arms and never let her go. "What do you think? Not too short, too clingy?"

Her face was flushed with pleasure. That expression on her face was the reason he'd planned this excursion. Alex had grown up with nothing, even when her parents were alive, and after, well, she'd worn other people's castoffs, and he remembered a time or two when she'd been forced to wear boys' clothes.

She'd been through a lot, had suffered unimaginable pain in her life. She deserved nothing but the best now, and he wanted to be the one to give it to her. He wanted to put that look of pleasure on her beautiful face every day. "You look spectacular. You take my breath away."

Alex's blush intensified, and his protective instincts fired to life. He wanted nothing more than to make her believe it. Make her see herself the way he saw her. She was a knockout in a designer dress, but she was just as stunning in a pair of cutoffs and a tank top.

She screwed up her face. "You think?"

He stepped closer, couldn't stop himself, and cupped her face. "You are—always have been—the most exquisite woman I have ever laid eyes on. You're beautiful, Alex, inside and out."

She shook her head, and her long dark hair slid over her shoulder, brushing the back of his hand. She inhaled deeply, eyes bright. "Deacon—"

"Alex?" Emily's voice came from behind him, and he cursed.

Seeing Alex looking like that, he'd momentarily forgotten his ex-wife and her friend were in the shop.

Alex's gaze darted over his shoulder and stuttered before she crossed her arms. "Wow...Emily, hey. Long time no see."

His ex strode forward, and he recognized the look in her eyes. This was the side of Emily that had eroded their relationship in the beginning.

"Well, I'll hand it to you, your persistence paid off. It looks like you got what you wanted in the end."

"Emily," he growled and stepped in front of Alex, blocking his ex's line of fire. "Do not say another damn word."

"God, you're so blind. I told you this morning, she's not good enough for you," Emily said in a surprisingly calm voice. "It's your money she's after. You know that, right?"

He heard Alex suck in a sharp breath behind him a second before she charged forward. "You spiteful cow."

He grabbed Alex around the waist and hauled her back.

"Have you finished?" he said to Emily, looking down at her and wondering what he'd ever seen in her. And how the hell he'd ever escape the twisted cycle they were locked in, allowing this woman to mess with his life. Emily shrugged, looking extremely pleased with herself. Her gaze moved to Alex, and she smirked.

When he turned to face Alex, he knew why. The look on her face terrified him, made his gut twist. *What are you thinking, baby?* Emily was a bitch, but Alex had dealt with far worse.

Jesus, he needed to get her away from these vultures. "Would you mind giving me a minute alone with Emily?" Alex didn't say a word, just pulled out of his arms and headed back to the dressing room. Her easy compliance alarmed him more than anything else.

"Oh, look, she's obedient as well," Tammy said.

He spun around and pinned his ex-wife's friend with a look that had silenced more than one asshole in the boardroom. "You're a nasty—"

"Deacon." Emily placed her hand on his arm and squeezed, successfully cutting him off. She stared up at him, the wounded innocence back, plastered on her face. It took all his control not to shake her off, shove her away. "I'm just worried about you, that's all, darling." Then she took her friend's arm and left the shop.

Fuck.

He wasn't quite sure what to do. Should he go in after Alex, explain? But what could he tell her? He had to keep Emily's secrets or risk the unthinkable. Despite their differences, what she'd done to him, he didn't want anything bad to happen to her. He sure as fuck refused to be the reason she took her own life. In the end he decided to stay put and wait it out. He knew Alex well enough to know she'd need a minute. If he went after her now, she'd retreat—her default when something didn't go to plan or she was hurt.

Alex came out a short time later, and thankfully the haunted expression was gone. "Well, that was fun."

He grabbed her upper arm and pulled her into his side. "I'm so sorry. I had no idea they'd be here."

"Why are you sorry? It wasn't you calling me a gold digger."

He tightened his hold, turning her so she faced him fully, and slid his fingers under her chin, tilting her head back so he could look in her eyes. "They don't know what they're talking about. They don't know you. Now let's forget about what just happened and get back to having a good time."

She crossed her arms. "Spending your money?"

"Don't." He held her gaze and hated the distance he saw there. "Do not let her get to you. That's exactly what she wanted."

"I'm fine." She held out her hand for her bag, and as he handed it back, accidentally upended it. "That's the last time I leave you to hold my purse."

Chuckling, he knelt beside her to help pick everything up. "You promise?"

She smiled, and relief washed over him. It was probably cheesy, but that's all he wanted. To make her smile. He was leaning forward, handing her her phone, when her gaze moved over his face and traveled down his throat to his chest. Her smile vanished.

"Alex?"

She reached out and yanked open the first two buttons of his shirt. He'd completely forgotten about the scratches on his chest. "It's not—"

"What I think?" She swallowed hard and looked down, shoving everything back in her purse. "You saw Emily this morning?"

"Yes, but—"

"She gave you those?"

"Yes, but—"

Alex stood abruptly, spun on her heel, and bolted for the door. "Alex, wait."

"Your things, Mr. West?" the shop assistant called after him.

"Send them to my office." Then he raced after Alex. She was striding down the street, shoulders and back stiff. He caught up, grabbed her arm, and spun her to face him. "Dammit, Alex, let me explain."

"Whatever. You and your ex screw from time to time." She shrugged. "I'd rather not hear the dirty details if you don't mind." She shoved out of his hold. "We also had a deal. No messing with anyone else, which means you forfeit and I win."

"Win? This isn't about..." He shook his head to clear his thoughts. "Right. I'm going to talk, and you're going to listen. Do you hear me?"

"I'm standing right here. I have ears. So yes, Deacon, I hear you. Whether or not I listen is another thing entirely."

"Would you cut the attitude for one damn minute?"

"Is that all you wanted to say?"

His brows shot up. "What the—"

"The answer is no. No, I will not cut the attitude."

"Alex." He made sure she heard the warning in his tone.

Martin pulled up at the curb beside them, and he could have hugged the man for following them.

"Deacon," she said in a deep mocking voice, mimicking him. "Well, did it work? Are you intimidated?"

The woman was driving him insane. "Can you get in the car, so I can explain?" She didn't move, just stared at him.

"Alex?"

"You didn't use the magic word," she said.

"Please."

She strode toward the car. "Fine, but only because I need a ride home."

He climbed in after her, but she wouldn't look at him. "So, Martin, how's it going?"

His poor frazzled driver looked stunned. "Ah, fine, thank you, Miss Franco."

"How's the family?"

"They're well. Thanks for asking."

"No problem."

"So, how long—"

"Alex," Deacon barked.

She stiffened and turned to him. "Well, that was rude. I was talking to Martin."

"Martin needs to concentrate on driving." He grabbed her and slid her across the seat so she was plastered to his side. She didn't struggle, she ignored him, and he realized that was so much worse. "Look at me." She stared out the window, continuing to ignore him completely. "Well, at least you've shut up long enough to listen."

She tensed against him, her outrage blatant.

"Yes, I did see Emily this morning. She came to my office uninvited, and when she confronted me about my interest in you, I told her the truth, that we were seeing each other. She didn't take it very well."

Alex spun to face him. "So what? You're telling me she attacked you like some wildcat because you're seeing someone else? She has a boyfriend, doesn't she? Why would she care who you're seeing?"

She didn't trust him, not in the slightest, and that pissed him off more than it should under the circumstances, especially with his own issues in that department. "Yes, she attacked me, and it wouldn't be the first time. The woman has a temper, and I've taken the brunt on more than one occasion."

"But why…" Alex turned more fully. "Deacon…"

"Do you believe me?"

She bit her lip and mulled over the simple question far too long for his liking. "I guess so."

"Either you do or you don't."

"Fine." She threw up her hands. "I believe you."

"Good." He brushed her silky dark hair off her shoulder and cupped the side of her throat, letting the smooth heat of her skin soothe him, calm his pounding heart. "I don't want to talk about her anymore."

"Fine with me."

He dragged her onto his lap and kissed her, slow and deep, letting her taste, her warmth calm him further. He pulled back, then kissed her once more because he had to. "I'm going to miss you while I'm away," he said, lips touching hers. She made a small noncommittal sound in the back of her throat.

She still didn't get it, still hadn't realized he didn't plan on letting her go. Ever.

But she would.

"You're the most stubborn woman I've ever met, you know that? And that's saying something with the sisters I have."

She laughed, soft and sweet, and his heart squeezed in response. "I'll take that as a compliment."

He rolled his eyes, purposely trying to bring back the fun from earlier in the day. "You would, you little tyrant."

"I take my job very seriously," she said, attempting to sound serious, but the glint in her eyes gave her away.

"Hmm, and what job is that?"

She nipped his lower lip, then sucked and licked the abused flesh, making him groan. "Driving you crazy."

He slid his hand over her ass and gave it a squeeze. "You need a pay raise then, because you're already a fucking expert."

She threw her head back and laughed, a full belly laugh that had him mesmerized. He couldn't take his eyes off her.

No, Alex Franco, I'm never letting you go.

Chapter Fifteen

Alex watched the Ford Mustang roll out of the parking lot and emptied her lungs in a rush. "Holy. Shit."

Rusty planted her hands on her slim hips and grinned at her, green eyes bright with excitement. "Can you freaking believe that?"

Alex shook her head, still stunned. "Nope. Maybe we're on a hidden camera show and some dude with a microphone's gonna jump out laughing his ass off and screaming, 'Suckers! We're only messing with you!'"

"This is what we were hoping for, what we said all along would happen, but still…" Rusty brushed her auburn hair back from her face. "Poaching one of R.I.P. Classic's customers? We get this one right…" She shook her head. "Shit, we'll be jumping in the deep end with the big boys."

Alex rubbed her suddenly sweaty palms on the sides of her shorts. "I think that's what it means, right?"

Rusty's spine straightened, determination transforming

her entire face, making her even more stunning, if that was possible. "That's exactly what it means. We screw this up, we might not get another chance. We have to kill it."

Alex bit her bit. "Right. No pressure then."

Rusty gave her a sharp nod. "Nope. None at all."

"Okay. Mr. Cannon's Charger should be ready for the painters day after tomorrow. Then you and me can concentrate on the Mustang, and Pipe can pull on a pair of coveralls and do the small jobs already booked in."

"Sounds good." Rusty looked down at her boots, and when she looked up her eyes were dancing, her grin barely contained. "We've so got this."

"We've more than got this. We fucking own it," Alex said, trying to keep a straight face.

"We'll fucking own it and spank its ass for good measure."

Alex crossed her arms and nodded. "We'll spank it till it purrs, force-feed it rocket fuel, then wheel spin that bitch into R.I.P. Classic's workshop, screaming, 'This is how we do it at West Restoration, bitches!'"

They gave up trying to keep it together after that and doubled over in a fit of nervous, hysterical laughter. They were still giggling when Piper came back with lunch.

She stopped in front of them, hands on hips, looking annoyed. "What did I miss this time?"

Alex and Rusty just laughed harder.

"Someone better tell me what's going on. I always miss the good stuff stuck in that goddamn office."

Alex slung her arm around Piper's shoulders. "Well, my friend, we're gonna need you to dust off your coveralls. That quote you did for the Mustang…"

"No," she whispered. "R.I.P. Classic's job. We didn't?"

"We did."

Piper's face lit up. Out of the three of them, she was the one with the best head for business, and lately had only been used occasionally in the workshop. They planned to change that when the place got busier. They'd hire a part-timer for the office and have Piper back out with them full-time, but they weren't there yet.

Rusty quickly filled Piper in.

"So I'm back in the workshop?" Pipe was beaming now.

"Yep."

"About damn time." She slid her arm around Alex's waist and gave her a squeeze. "I was starting to worry if I didn't get some grease on my hands again soon, I'd morph into Deacon."

Rusty tugged on her sister's blond ponytail. "God, I hope not. One suited control freak in the family is enough, thank you very much. Besides, having to shave every day would seriously put the brakes on your love life."

At the mention of Deacon, a rush of guilt and longing moved through Alex at the speed of light. She hated keeping secrets from her friends, but what choice did she have? They wouldn't understand—how could they? And if she was honest with herself, she knew this was the only way to work Deke out of her system. Their night together six months ago hadn't let her go, no matter how hard she'd tried to forget it, forget *him*. At least this way, they both got what they wanted.

Piper snorted as they headed to the office. "What love life?"

They took their seats around Piper's desk while she handed out sandwiches. Rusty slumped back in her chair. "Yeah, the only one getting laid around here is Alex." She waggled her eyebrows and took a massive bite of her ham and cheese on rye. "How is Jarrod?"

Piper slapped her sister's knee. "Gross. No wonder you're not getting laid with table manners like that. Don't talk with your damn mouth full."

Ah, crap. "Yeah, fine."

"Fine?" Piper shook her head. "Oh, no, you don't. We want details. This is the first serious boyfriend you've had. So spill. And don't skimp on the details. I have to live vicariously through you." She scowled at her sister.

Piper had a record for picking total losers, or assholes who decided they liked her big sister a whole lot more. So Deke and Rusty took it upon themselves to terrify the crap out of any man who showed an interest in their baby sister, testing them. They had to prove their worth if they wanted to date her. Poor, sweet-natured Piper didn't stand a chance.

They were both staring at her, waiting for her to spill her guts. Jesus. She had to give them something. "It's just casual, you know? Just sex."

"Mmm-hmm." Rusty was wearing her I-see-all expression, which meant she was in serious trouble. "How good is the sex, then? Must be pretty spectacular to hook up as much as you and the suit have this last week. You're hardly home."

She took a bite of her sandwich and chewed slowly, stalling. "I guess."

Rusty grinned. "Well, is the dude hung or what?"

Alex was in the middle of drinking her soda and sucked her mouthful down the wrong way. Piper jumped up and pounded on her back. Alex scowled at Rusty, who was now giggling her ass off.

Her friend shrugged. "What? Piper wants to know as well."

"She does not." Giving her friends intimate details of their brother's anatomy did not sit well with her. Not at all. They'd be scarred for life if they ever found out.

"Well, yeah, I kinda do," Piper said as she took her seat again.

Alex stood and stomped to the door. "Enough talk about my sex life. Go get one of your own." She pulled the door open. "And if you ask me how *hung* he is one more time, I'll stick dead rats in both your beds."

There. Ha! She spun around and slammed on the breaks, mouth dropping open. A customer stood there, eyes round as saucers. "Shit. Um…I mean…what I meant to say was…" She took a steadying breath. "Your car's ready, Mr. Porter. Please follow me."

Her friends' barely restrained laughter followed her as she went to grab the guy's keys.

The rest of the afternoon was thankfully busy and blessedly uneventful, so Alex wasn't forced to endure any further questions. This was getting complicated already, and they hadn't even reached the two-week mark.

And it wasn't only Piper and Rusty asking questions that had her second-guessing what she was doing. That confrontation with Emily and Tammy. Alex cringed inwardly, remembered humiliation heating her cheeks. They thought she was nothing but a gold-digging slut, and why not? She and Deacon were worlds apart now. They knew as well as she did that a man like Deacon would never want anything but a fling with someone like her.

It had shaken her. The way they saw her, the way

everyone would see her when she and Deke were together. She would never fit into his world, and she refused to change for any man. Even Deacon. Huffing out a breath, she shook her head. The point was moot anyway. That wasn't what they were about.

And why did she care what a couple of stuck-up Barbies thought of her, anyway?

She dropped her wrench into the toolbox, wiped her hands off on a rag, and stuffed it in her back pocket. Then, closing the hood of the car she was working on, she walked around, reached through the driver's side window, and twisted the key in the ignition, turning the engine over.

The car roared to life. At least one thing was going right.

She threw a cover over the driver's seat to protect the upholstery and climbed in. The deep growl of the 1967 Plymouth 'Cuda's V8 rumbled through the seat, right through her. Nothing beat it. As long as she had Rusty and Piper, the garage, she could handle anything. Even losing Deacon when their three months were up.

She had to believe that.

Putting the car in first, she rolled out of the garage and onto the street to take it for a test run. Window down, the wind tugged at her ponytail, the sun warming her skin. Yeah, this was all she needed.

Then Emily's nasty face entered her head again.

Shit. She needed to stop second-guessing herself. But dammit, why did Deacon put up with his ex interfering in his life anyway? He and Emily were divorced. He promised there was nothing going on between them. So what was it? It was like Emily had some kind of hold over him. When she'd seen the scratches on Deke's chest, she'd felt sick to her stomach, and yeah, she'd overreacted. But in that moment, the past had reared up and smacked her upside the head. Emily was a bitch, but she was also poised, beautiful, classy—and the woman Deacon had chosen over her. The woman he'd chosen to marry. The woman he still had a relationship with. Seeing them together, she'd felt like she had back then, when he'd left her behind to be with Emily. Not good enough.

Never good enough.

But in the end, she had no choice but to believe him. Why would he lie?

Still, she couldn't get her head around it. If it was truly over between them, then why let her insinuate herself in his life like she seemed to? Why not tell her to piss off and mind her own damn business? She hadn't missed the way he held back around his ex-wife, treated her with kid gloves. It didn't make any sense unless...

She shook her head and turned up the stereo to flush out the thoughts bombarding her. She refused to waste another minute thinking about that woman.

When she drove back twenty minutes later, she got a raised eyebrow from Rusty as she pulled to a stop in the workshop. "You get lost?"

"Engine trouble," she said, lying through her teeth.

She'd needed longer than a spin around the block to clear her head. Deke would be back tonight, and she needed to get her shit together before she saw him again. She'd missed him more than she should. After only one night, a restless, lonely feeling had taken up residence in her chest. And when he'd called to say things were taking longer than he'd anticipated and he would be away another night, her disappointment had been acute.

Those pale green eyes narrowed. "You got it sorted now?"

"I hope so." Pulling the keys from the ignition to lock in the safe for the night, she climbed out.

Rusty stopped her before she'd taken two steps. "You'd tell me if something was bothering you, right?"

Alex swallowed hard, mouth suddenly dry. "Yeah, Rust." Jesus, she hated this. "You know I would." Rusty gave her a small nod, then they both got busy cleaning up for the night.

As guilty as she felt for lying to her best friends, and as much as she tried to fight it, she was helpless against the rush of excitement that moved through her when she realized in a few hours Deacon would be knocking on her front door.

She was so screwed.

Chapter Sixteen

It was late when Deacon pulled in behind West Restoration. His meeting had run late. Usually he would have just stayed out of town another night, but it turned out, two days away from Alex was more than he could handle.

He'd called, told her he wouldn't make dinner, but she'd promised to wait up for him. The breathlessness to her voice when he spoke to her, that husky edge of hers, had near done him in. That alone had driven him to get in his car, to drive straight over here, despite the hour. He needed her. And he sure as hell wouldn't leave her wanting.

Going away, especially after what happened with Emily, had not been ideal. He'd wanted nothing more than to take Alex home and show her how much he cared, convince her to trust him, to forget their snide comments. Hell, he'd needed it for himself—the doubt on her face, the hurt she'd tried to hide had nearly killed him.

Climbing out of his car, he walked around the side of

the workshop, where he'd hidden his car, and looked over to his sisters' cottage. The place was dark—both had turned in for the night. He glanced up and saw pale yellow light illuminated the front windows of Alex's apartment. Thank God.

Being Alex's landlord meant he had a key to her place, and he'd told her to lock up, that he'd let himself in. He took the external stairs to her front door and used his key.

"Alex?" He shut the door behind him and moved into the kitchen. No sign of her.

But when he moved into the small adjoining living room, he saw her. On her side, hand tucked under her chin, asleep on the couch. Jesus, he'd missed her more than he thought possible. The more time they spent together, the more of herself she revealed, the deeper his already intense feelings became.

She was wearing nothing but a baggy Guns N' Roses tank top that skimmed the tops of her thighs and looked unbelievably sexy. Her smooth, bare legs were stretched out, toenails painted blue, and right then, he thought the cute silver toe ring she wore might be the hottest thing he'd ever seen. The woman was temptation and innocence all at the same time.

She also looked utterly wiped out.

As badly as he wanted her, he didn't have the heart to wake her. He knew firsthand what a restless sleeper she could be. What those dreams did to her, how they shook her. She looked so peaceful. Cursing under his breath, he thrust his fingers through his hair. He could wait till tomorrow, right? One more night wouldn't kill him.

Fuck.

Her scent, unique to Alex, spicy and exotic, filled the small apartment and hit him in the gut. The roar of need increased along with the swirl of emotion only Alex had managed to evoke in him. He needed to leave before he changed his mind and acted like the selfish bastard she already thought he was.

Walking to the kitchen as quietly as he could, he grabbed a pen and jotted down a note so she knew he hadn't stood her up, then took the blanket off the back of the couch and placed it over her. He took one last long look at his sleeping beauty and let himself out.

Every step away from her felt heavy, wrong on every level, but he knew how hard they'd all been working. West Restoration had begun to make a name for itself, and he would never stand in the way of their success, despite what he'd told Alex.

When he reached the bottom step, his gaze moved to the workshop's side door, and that old familiar pain lanced through his chest.

God, the way he'd felt going to his father that day, the pain that had sliced across his old man's face when he'd told him what he'd seen. Deacon had thought he was doing the right thing. He'd been angry and hurt, and still in shock, after finding his mother with another man. Jacob West had been heartbroken, humiliated. His own son discovering what he hadn't seen himself was too much for his pride to recover from.

His parents separated after that, and he and his father had begun to drift apart. Maybe his mother would have left on her own, eventually, maybe she wouldn't. He'd opened his mouth, and because of that, his dad had lost the woman he loved and his sisters had grown up without their mother. He'd blamed himself. As he'd gotten older, his relationship with his father had only gone from bad to worse.

But when he dropped the bomb that he was going to business school instead of working at the garage and one day taking it over—things had completely fallen apart. They'd never recovered from it. Never made their peace, and now it was too late.

Before he realized what he was doing, he had the keys for Alex's apartment in his hand. Spare keys for the garage and the cottage were on the key ring as well, and he unlocked the door. The place was pitch-black, but he knew every square foot; it was as familiar to him as the back of his own hand. He went straight to the security system flashing beside the door and disengaged the alarm, then, shutting the door behind him, flicked on the overhead lights.

This place. The smell. The memories. He'd had some of the best times of his life in this workshop. He'd also suffered some of the worst. The fight with his father that he'd been too damn stubborn to forget. He'd held onto every angry word and let it fuel him, push him to succeed, to show his father how wrong he was, that he could make something of himself.

So much wasted time.

Shoving the keys in his pocket, he moved across the concrete floor to the back of the room. There in the far corner, covered in canvas to keep off the dust, was his father's 1965 Pontiac GTO. Jacob had left it to him in his will, along with this building. He wasn't stupid enough to miss the significance. It was an apology. His father's way of saying, "I'm sorry." He'd left in Deacon's hands the care and protection of those things most precious to him. His beloved car and, more importantly, the welfare of his daughters and their maddening best friend.

It was too late to say he was sorry, but he'd make sure his sisters—and Alex—were taken care of.

The old bastard always did get the last word.

Gripping the heavy canvas, he dragged it back, revealing the old girl in all her glory. The car was exquisite. Jacob had done it all himself, every inch painstakingly restored. Giving this to Deacon was as good as an *I love you, son. I'm proud of you.* Two things he'd been desperate to hear for such a long time. They'd let their stupid pride keep them apart, and he was still struggling with the guilt six months later. Which was why the car was still here and not in the parking garage under his apartment.

Running his hand over the sleek cherry-red paint, he smiled as memories flooded him. Him and his sisters, Alex. All the kids piled in the thing, waiting to go for a spin. Jacob telling them to wash their hands. "No food or drink in my baby," he always barked before they headed out.

The sound of someone coming down the stairs washed away the memory, and he turned in time to see Alex walking through the door.

She smiled when she saw him—it was hesitant, almost shy, and the most beautiful thing he'd ever seen. "I found your note." She held it up and waved it around.

"So I see. How did you know I was still here?"

"I saw your car out my bedroom window." She crossed her arms. "Why didn't you wake me?"

He swallowed past the lump in his throat and fought to hold his ground, not to grab her then and there and show her just how much he'd missed her. "You looked so peaceful. I didn't have the heart." She moved out from behind the car that had been concealing the lower half of her body, and he nearly swallowed his tongue. "You, ah…you got the boots then?"

She nodded. "Yup. I woke up to find them on my doorstep the morning after you left. Poor Martin must have gotten up at the crack of dawn to get them to me unnoticed."

She kept moving toward him. That Guns N' Roses tank, now that she was standing, was still barely long enough to cover her panties. And those boots, the ones he'd seen her drooling over, the ones he'd wanted to see her in and nothing else, looked amazing, like he knew they would. His cock was hard as iron, straining against the zipper of his trousers. "Do you like them?"

She shook her head. "Nope." Then a wicked grin tilted up one side of those lush lips. "I love them."

The woman was capable of running circles around him, fucking owned him and didn't even realize it. "Stop," he rasped. "Not another step." Her brows shot up, but she did what he asked. He spun his finger in a circle, silently asking her to turn around for him, and to his delight she complied without question. "Stunning."

Her back was to him, but he didn't miss her soft moan. His little viper was as hot for him as he was for her. Unable to keep his hands off her another minute, he moved up behind her and rested his hands on the gentle flare of her hips. "I've been fantasizing about you in those boots ever since you picked them up."

"You have?"

She sounded breathless, needy, and it cranked up his

own need. He was too far gone, had missed her too much to wait. Gripping the hem of her tank, he lifted it over her head and tossed it on the roof of the car. She sucked in a startled breath. "Oh, yes." He coasted his fingers over bare skin, across her ribs, and up to her firm breasts. A perfect handful. He massaged the soft mounds, pinching her nipples, tugging gently on her sensitive flesh.

"Deke...please," she whispered.

He kissed the side of her neck and sucked the smooth skin, marking her. "I'm sorry, baby. Sorry I couldn't get back to you like I promised." He trailed a hand down over her taut stomach, the muscles quivering under his palm, and dipped his fingers beneath the elastic of her deep blue lace panties, groaning when he felt slick, wet heat. "You need it, don't you, Alex?"

She shifted her hips, trying to get him to move his fingers. "Yes."

"You've missed my cock, my mouth, the whole time I was gone, haven't you?" He slid his finger through her folds and up to circle her clit.

Her head dropped back against his chest, and she whimpered. "Yes."

God, she was amazing, so responsive to his touch, holding back nothing. "Did you touch yourself while I was gone, baby?"

"Yes," she gasped.

Jesus. He pressed his cock into the soft curve of her ass to relieve the throbbing pressure, and when he spoke again his voice was so deep with raw lust, he barely recognized it. "Did you think of me when you came? When your fingers pushed inside that tight, sweet body, was it my fingers you were imagining?"

"Yes."

He groaned and pulled his hand free of her underwear so he could spin her around. She made a small sound of protest before he slammed his mouth down on hers, desperate to taste her. He thrust his tongue inside the wet heat of her mouth, and she returned his kiss wildly. She tasted of peppermint and that unique taste that was all Alex, a taste that was branded into his senses, a taste he had never forgotten, not since their first kiss all those years ago.

Gripping her waist, he lifted her off the ground, and she wrapped her legs around his hips instantly. He couldn't wait to have her and sat her on the hood of the Pontiac. Her hair was wild around her face and shoulders, eyes glazed and heavy with lust as he pushed his fingers down the sides of her underwear. "Lift up." She leaned back on her hands and lifted her ass so he could slide her panties down her legs, and he flung them on the roof of the car with her tank top.

Her breathing had increased, warm puffs bursting past her kiss-swollen lips. "This is what I've been fantasizing about." He reached down and pressed his palm against the aching ridge of his erection. "This is the image that has kept me hard since I saw you looking at these boots."

She squeezed her thighs together and whimpered.

"Are you aching, Alex?"

"Yes."

"Show me what you did to yourself while I was away, and I'll give you a reward." He was torturing himself, but fuck it. Just knowing that she'd gotten herself off thinking of him was making him crazy. Her eyes flared, and she bit her lip. "Do it. Touch yourself. Show me."

She kept those amazing eyes on him as she slid a hand down over her belly and between her spread thighs. He swallowed hard as she spread herself with delicate fingers and started slicking her arousal up and back.

"Jesus Christ," he hissed, closer to losing it than he had been in his entire life. "That's it, sweetheart. Make yourself come. Get yourself off while I watch."

She made a needy little whimper and pushed a finger inside her tight opening, gasping, undulating her hips. He knew her eyes were locked on him, he could feel it, but he couldn't tear his gaze away from what she was doing between her thighs. Her fingers pumped in and out, rapidly, glistening with her wetness. Then she pulled out, slid them to her clit, and started circling. Her whimpers got louder, more desperate, then she was coming, crying out, body shaking.

"Fucking stunning." He'd never been closer to disgracing himself in his entire life. She'd collapsed back, breathing heavily. He took her hand lying limp on her thigh and lifted it to his mouth, sucking her fingers clean, and his cock pulsed harder. "You need more?"

"Yes," she whispered.

"Do you want me to make it all better?"

"Please. Please make it better."

She was killing him. Alex never begged for anything, never showed vulnerability—she'd always seen it as a weakness, an opportunity for others to take advantage. But right now she wasn't holding anything back from him. It was all there in her expressive dark eyes. Things she would never say out loud, things that had his heart pounding in his chest.

"Spread your legs wider, sweetheart. Show me how hot and wet you are." She let her parted knees fall open, giving him what he asked for. He groaned, so desperate to slam inside her he was fucking shaking. He slid his fingers around her left ankle and hooked the heel of one boot behind the car's big chrome grill, then the other. "I want to slide my tongue inside that tight little snatch so bad I can barely think straight, but you need my cock, don't you, baby?"

She made a hot, hungry sound in the back of her throat. "Yes."

She was completely exposed, open to him, at his mercy. "Do you have any idea how exquisite you look right now?" He ran his hands up her inner thighs, opening her farther. "This is another fantasy of mine, actually. Though this one's been around a lot longer." He massaged her inner thighs, not giving her what she wanted, what they both wanted, just yet.

Her breath hitched. "Tell me."

Jesus. He'd spent more nights than he could remember before and after the first time he'd slept with Alex thinking of this. Nights when he was forced to rub off hard and fast, biting his pillow so no one would hear him groaning out her name.

"I spent a lot of time imagining you just like this, naked, at my mercy." He moved his hand higher, cupping her. *Shit, so hot.* And gently massaged her slick flesh. She bucked her hips, gasping. "Fucking you hard on the hood of one of these old cars. But in my fantasy, we're out in the country. The sun's beating down, warming all that smooth skin. You're calling my name, begging me to take you harder, and I do, I take you so hard you scream and come around my cock. Do you want that, Alex? You want me to fuck you hard?"

Chapter Seventeen

Alex was mindless at this point. Nothing but need and desperation.

"You want me to fuck you hard?" Deacon repeated, hand still between her thighs, teasing her, making her quiver and shake. She was sensitive from making herself come and on the verge of coming again just from his gentle touch, the sound of his voice. His rough commands and descriptions of what he wanted to do to her.

"Yes. I want it." She ignored the begging note to her voice, or how much letting him take control over her in this way turned her on. How much she needed it from him. With Deacon, she could just let go.

He started undoing the buttons on his shirt, and she realized he must have come to her straight from the airport. He'd taken off the jacket but was still wearing trousers instead of jeans. For some reason the thought of him rushing straight to her, coming to her first, made her belly flutter. He balled up his shirt and threw it on the car with her tank top, then dropped his hands to the front of his pants.

Yes, please. Her inner muscles fluttered in anticipation as he undid his belt and shoved down his pants and boxers, freeing that beautiful, long cock. He didn't take his eyes off her as he moved between her trembling thighs. One of his hands landed on her waist, the other moving up to cup the side of her throat, his fingers lingering over her hammering pulse.

He sucked in an unsteady breath. "You are so beautiful, Alex." His hand moved down between her breasts, over her belly. "You don't have any idea, do you?"

His voice was deep, rough, had a note of something she was afraid to believe in, afraid to hope for. Just afraid, full stop. The intensity in his gaze made it hard to hold his stare. *What the hell is he doing?*

It was too much, not enough. She needed him to stop looking at her like that. She needed to bring this back to the reason she was lying naked on the hood of his father's Pontiac. Bringing her hands to her breasts, she teased her nipples. "Don't make me beg for it, Deke. Come on. Give it to me." The muscles in her thighs shook, her body way past want to flat-out need at this point.

His nostrils flared. "Oh, I'm going to give it to you," he rasped.

But instead of slamming inside her, taking her hard like he'd promised, he positioned himself and slid deep inside her, nice and slow. When he was fully seated, he leaned over her and kissed her. The kiss was deep, tender, and had the ability to break her into a thousand pieces.

No. No. No. Not this, anything but this. She reached down

and gripped his ass, grinding against his hips. He squeezed his eyes shut for a moment, sucking in deep steadying breaths. Dammit, she wanted him to lose control. To take her like he had in the bar, over her kitchen table. Taking her hands, he gripped them in one of his and lifted them over her head, holding her completely immobile.

He stared down at her. "Not this time, sweetheart. This time we're going to take it slow."

She started to shake her head in denial, panic knotting her lower belly, but then he withdrew, and she moaned at the feel of all that hard, hot flesh moving inside her. He was relentless, his big body shaking with the effort, but the stubborn bastard took his time, kissing her in a way that made her heart hurt, made her wish for things that could never be. Didn't he realize what he was doing to her? What this was doing to her?

"Fuck, I missed this," he rasped against her lips.

Jesus. She couldn't take much more.

He grunted, soft and deep, and kept on making the unconscious, unrestrained sound every time he pushed inside her. It was the sexiest thing she'd ever heard; it lifted the hair on the back of her neck, made her toes curl.

"I missed the feel of you, so tight around my cock, the way you grasp me tighter when I pull out like you can't bear me to leave. You need this as badly as me, don't you, sweetheart?"

"Yes." The word came out with her next breath, before she could swallow it down.

His gaze blazed, the muscles under her hands jumping. His thrusts intensified, still at the same slow pace, but deeper, harder. "I love the way your lips part when I push inside, the way your breath hitches," he rasped.

Oh, God. He was killing her.

He continued to make love to her, never taking his eyes off her, following the cues of her body to take her higher.

She shivered and closed her eyes against all that intensity staring down at her.

"Look at me," he demanded.

Helpless to do anything but obey at this point, she lifted her lids.

"I want you to see what you do to me. How good you make me feel." He reached down and cupped her ass, tilting her hips up, then thrust back in, grinding against her. She sobbed, so close, so damn close. "Only you make me feel this way, Alex, this hungry, this possessive." He repeated the slow thrust and grind and the pressure increased. "You make me crazy, sweetheart. Wild. Only you do that to me. No one else."

His abs tightened as he bent to suck the bar piercing her nipple, drawing it into his mouth, then thrust deep and held her there. One more tug on her nipple, and she shattered, hard. When he lifted up, covering her body, she hung on tight, sinking her teeth into the firm muscle of his shoulder to stop from screaming. He started to move then, no more slow torture; now he pounded into her, arms locked around her, holding her immobile. All she could do was take it, lie there and absorb the full power of his lust. Lost in the sound of his grunts of pleasure, the rough, tender words he rasped against her ear, drawing out her own orgasm, she clung to him in return, never wanting him to let her go.

Then with a shout he came hard inside her, big body tensing and shaking through his release.

Collapsing over her, he pressed her into the now warm, unyielding steel at her back, but she didn't care. Nothing had ever felt so good, so right. She smoothed her hands over his wide shoulders as he glided in and out of her slow and easy, and she knew there would be no returning from this. She was completely lost to him, always had been. And for the first time in her life, she wanted to take a risk on loving someone, despite the possibility of losing him.

She blinked hard when her eyes started to sting and swallowed against the lump in her throat when it threatened to escape in a painful sob.

Damn you, Deacon. Damn you for making me love you.

• • •

Alex miraculously found a parking spot right outside Deacon's apartment building. Probably because the sun was barely up.

She'd gotten up early—they had another busy day ahead, and she wanted to talk to him before it was time to open the garage.

Nerves flipped around in her belly. This was a stupid idea, wasn't it? Maybe she'd lost her mind.

She hadn't been thinking straight, not since Deacon had carried her upstairs and tucked her in bed after making love to her.

I hate leaving you, Alex. I know I'll see you in a few hours, but I already miss you.

He'd whispered the words against her hair, kissed her, then left. She'd hated it, too. But it was too risky for him to stay, and they both knew it. Still, when she'd watched him walk out the door, she'd had to bite her lip so she didn't beg him to stay.

Last night she realized she wanted to be more than his fuck buddy, more than an arrangement. A man didn't look at a woman like Deacon looked at her, didn't make slow, sweet love to a woman like he had her, and not care about that woman, right?

Only you make me feel this way, Alex, this hungry, this possessive.

She shivered at the memory. He'd claimed her last night. She'd felt it in every fiber of her being. Everything had changed, everything. She had no idea what it meant going forward. Deacon had made it clear at the beginning he didn't want a relationship, that what they had going on had a use-by date. Did he still feel that way after last night?

No. She couldn't believe it. He made sure she felt wanted, desired...important.

Alex was a lot of things, but a coward wasn't one of them. There was too much at stake—her heart, for one. Her friendship with his sisters and their garage for another. If there was a chance for them, if he wanted the same thing she did, they needed to forget about their arrangement and just...be together.

Was she really going to do this? What choice did she have? She couldn't go on like this. She'd been stupid, naive to think she could.

Blowing out a deep breath, she reached over and grabbed the coffees she'd bought on the way, climbed out of her Viper, and headed into the building. The doorman was already at his post and gave her a warm smile when he opened up for her. "Hey, Harold."

He tipped his hat and smiled. "Morning, miss."

Blood was pounding through her veins, and her knees felt weak and shaky as she crossed the floor. This was a huge risk. God, what if she was wrong? What if he didn't feel the same way she did? She shook her head, fought the self-doubt back. Deke had changed over the years. No, he wasn't the same boy she'd first fallen for. He was a man. The type of man who went after what he wanted ruthlessly. He didn't let anyone get in his way. Well, she could learn a thing or two from him in that respect.

And despite it all, despite the suits, the flashy cars, and the expensive apartment, he was still her Deke. He was still in there. He'd shown himself time and again over the last couple weeks. That tender, caring, protective side was still in there under the hard exterior, and she had to believe he couldn't do what they were doing and not feel something for her other than lust.

The elevator door opened, and a guy strode out. It was the same guy from the first night she'd been here, the night she'd bolted from Deacon's apartment as soon as he'd fallen asleep. Sitting in the foyer, barefoot and more than likely looking like a woman who'd recently been screwing her brains out.

Averting her gaze, she tried to slip past, but he touched her arm. "Hey, I know you, right? You were here a couple weeks ago? I remember the ink." His gaze darted to her arm, to the rose tattoo poking out from under her sleeve.

She tensed. "And?"

"And you were hard to miss." The guy moved in close, and she had no choice but to take a step back or he'd be all up in her personal space. "I was hoping I'd see you again.

Can I have a word?"

"Nope. I have somewhere to be." She went to move past again, but he took the drinks from her hands and placed them on the unmanned reception desk near the elevator. "What the hell?"

He straightened his tie and gave her a lopsided grin. "I think you might be interested in what I have to say. I've been looking for someone in your line of business, actually, but haven't found the right fit, so to speak. I think you and I might get on just fine."

Unease turned to relief, then excitement. Deacon must have told him about West Restoration, which meant he obviously knew the guy. She shrugged off the way her creep-o-meter was wailing and joined him by the reception desk. "Look, I know the competition in this city is fierce, but I promise you won't be disappointed. I've never had a dissatisfied customer. In fact, they always come back." She was no Rusty when it came to this stuff—that woman had the gift of gab—but she was no slouch.

His gaze dropped to her breasts, and she automatically crossed her arms. Maybe he just liked Iron Maiden? The T-shirt was old and fitted. She glanced down and her face heated when she realized crossing her arms caused the fabric to cling and show off the outline of her barbell.

"God, that's so sexy. Damn." He moved closer. "What's your rate, sweetheart?"

Her ease vanished, and her empty stomach churned. "It depends on what you want done," she answered cautiously.

"I want a whole night. Maybe a regular thing? I get the feeling one night with you wouldn't be enough. Deacon West keeps coming back for more, so you must be worth whatever your fee is."

He thinks I'm a prostitute? He touched her hip, and she shoved him back. "You are way the hell out of line."

She tried to move past him, but he grabbed her arm, crowded her. "Don't be like that. You want to be wined and dined first? I can do that. My money's just as good as West's."

Before she had the chance to knee him in the balls, he was being wrenched back, arms windmilling to prevent himself from falling on his ass. Deacon, looking like he was capable of murder, wrapped his hand around the other guy's throat and shoved him against the nearest wall. "You touch her again, and I will kill you. Do you understand?"

The guy screwed his face up. "You want the whore all to yourself, you can have her. Plenty more where she came from."

Murder flashed in Deacon's eyes.

"Deacon. No!"

He completely ignored her, pulled back, and slammed his fist into the creep's face. The crunch of bone shattering made her wince, as did the blood that splattered across Deacon's white shirt.

The guy howled and covered his nose. "Jesus Christ! You broke my nose!"

Deacon ignored him and turned to her. "Elevator, now."

When she stood unmoving, still in shock, he grabbed her arm and dragged her along with him, pulling her in before the door closed. "What the hell, Deacon?"

His jaw was granite, and when he looked down at her there was no warmth or affection in his hard gaze. He didn't speak, not until they were in his apartment, after he'd dragged her into his bedroom. She stood on the opposite side while he tugged his shirt from his trousers, undid the first few buttons, and pulled it over his head, throwing it across the room.

"One man not enough for you, Alex?"

The emotion behind his words felt like a physical blow. Anger she could handle, though she sure as hell didn't deserve it. But it wasn't just anger radiating from him—no, there was pain as well. And the expression on his face twisted her up inside.

"I come down to find you with that asshole..." He shoved a hand through his hair. "After last... After what we..." He growled, shook his head.

After last night? Was that what he was going to say? She crossed her arms over her chest, more hurt and angry than she'd been in her life, which should be impossible, but there you go. How could he still doubt her? "I was not with that asshole, he followed me."

"Yeah?" The raw emotion in his voice had not diminished, not even a fraction.

She moved closer to him, her own anger sailing over pissed and landing somewhere in the vicinity of rage. Deacon wasn't the only one hurting. His opinion of her, as it turned out, wasn't much better than that bastard downstairs. But despite her desire to lash out, to rail on him, she kept her voice controlled, even. "You get that in my line of work."

His hands clenched and unclenched at his sides as she moved in, so close her breasts brushed his chest. "What the hell are you talking about?"

"Whore, Deacon." He visibly flinched, mouth opening, then closing. "Your friend downstairs wanted to know my hourly rate."

A flush crept up from his neck, and he gritted his teeth. "What did you just say?"

"Do you really need me to spell it out? Here, maybe I should show you." She yanked on his belt, pulling the leather free, unbuckling it to shove her hand inside. She was surprised when she found him hard as iron, cock pulsing in her hand.

"What are you doing?" He grabbed her wrists, holding them firmly in his.

"I would have thought that was obvious. Services rendered and all that. Maybe you'd prefer my mouth?" She tried to drop to her knees in front of him, but he released her hands and gripped her upper arms, holding her immobile. "I thought you loved it when I sucked your cock?"

His nostrils flared, and the heat in his gaze sent her up in flames, but he didn't release his hold, nor did the anger causing his body to shake diminish.

She tried to fight him, tried to drop down in front of him again. "Suddenly you've grown a conscience? What, don't tell me you *care* for your little whore, Deacon?"

She hadn't meant to say that. Still her pulse raced, wanting to hear it, to hear that he actually gave a shit.

Instead he stood there like a damn robot, confusion and God only knew what else in his gaze, looking at her like she'd grown a second head. Oh, yeah, he knew the ugly truth as well as she did. They could never be together. They were from different worlds now. She'd momentarily forgotten that, had let her emotions cloud her better judgment. Convinced herself their feelings for each other would be enough to overcome their differences, that they were so much more than what they were.

What she was.

But even if Deacon had considered more, some kind of future together that didn't include sneaking around—well, the reality of his neighbor soliciting sex from her would have knocked any stupid ideas from his head.

Having a girlfriend who could pass as a streetwalker? Not a good look for a corporate CEO.

She pulled out of his arms, and he let her. Let her pace to the other side of the room, away from him. Pain more acute than she thought possible gripped her heart.

"Alex..." He took a step toward her, then slammed on the brakes, shoved his fingers through his hair, and bit off several more curses.

I am such an idiot.

Tears stung the backs of her eyes, but she refused to let him see her cry. Goddammit, she would not fall apart in front of him. She darted through the closest door, into the bathroom, and shut herself in. Sucking down several deep breaths, she fought to keep her emotions in check. *You knew this would happen, but you still opened your heart. This is your own damn fault. Stupid. Stupid. Stupid.*

Head bent, she stared at the floor, then her gaze landed on the trash basket. A shirt had been dumped in there, and she could see something pink smudged on it. Without thinking, she lifted it out and held it up.

Lipstick stained the front pocket and one side of the collar. *Oh, God.* She stood frozen. It sure as hell wasn't hers. But it didn't take a mind like Sherlock Holmes to figure out who the owner of the lipstick was, either.

Had he kept Emily on the sidelines all along?

She shook her head. If she believed that, she was no

better than Deke, with his mistrust and accusations. There had to be a reasonable explanation, didn't there?

God, she wanted to believe that, so much, but that old fear—the sting of his rejection when he'd left her for Emily—lurked below the surface, making it hard to think clearly.

All of a sudden she was suffocating. Every breath seemed to scald her throat, her lungs shrinking in her chest with each painful breath. She threw the shirt back in the trash and bolted from the bathroom.

"Alex?" Deacon called after her.

"I need to get back to work." He came after her, grabbed her arms, and stupid hope fluttered through her belly. She turned to face him but couldn't read the expression on his face.

"Don't run away from me, Alex. Not again."

"I have to go." She tried to pull free, but he held on tight. "Let me go." She barely recognized her own voice, so broken, so damn pathetic.

He winced a second before his expression closed down completely.

Then he did what she asked—he released her, stepped back, and let her walk out the door.

Chapter Eighteen

Deacon gripped the steering wheel tight enough to make it groan as he pulled into the parking garage under his apartment building. After an afternoon spent explaining to his goddamn lawyer why he'd broken that bastard's nose, his shitty mood still hadn't improved. The asshole would more than likely sue.

It was worth it.

At the end of the day, it was only money. And that bastard more than deserved what he'd gotten.

He still didn't know what had come over him. He'd lost it. In his surprise at seeing Alex there, then the way the guy had crowded her, put his hands on her. Like an idiot, he'd immediately thought the worst. His default after Emily's deceit, her cheating. The way his mother had done the same to his father.

Trusting another person, even Alex, didn't come easily. But she hadn't deserved his rancor, his accusations.

Don't tell me you care *for your little whore, Deacon?*

Jesus. He'd frozen when she'd fired those pain-filled words at him. The realization of what he'd done, what he'd accused her of when he knew better, knew she would never do that to him, had hit hard.

She'd called herself a whore. *He'd* made her feel that way. She doubted his feelings for her. Had no clue how he felt. That knowledge had rendered him speechless. And so fucking ashamed of the way he'd treated her, the things he'd said. Buried in his own petty jealousy, he had struggled with what he could possibly do or say to make it right.

So he'd done fucking nothing.

He'd messed up.

God, her face—he'd literally seen her pulling away from him, shutting down, and he'd imploded. Too many emotions warring to take front and center. In the end, he'd been unable to convey anything but anger. Furious with that asshole, and furious with himself for causing her to doubt her feelings for him, feelings she hadn't been able to hide the night before when he'd made love to her.

But what pissed him off most of all was that he'd allowed his past to get in the way of what he could have with Alex. Instead of helping her work through her fears, he'd allowed his own, his fear of losing her, to take over. He'd messed things up. Again.

So much so, he'd managed to obliterate any progress he'd made with her, the trust he'd worked so hard to gain.

And she'd run from him.

He slammed his hands down on the steering wheel and shoved the door open. Screw it. He was supposed to attend a business meeting tonight with Alex, but he'd cancel. He needed time with her alone, to try to repair the damage he'd done.

Did she truly believe he saw her as nothing but a whore? Jesus, the idea made him ill. Yeah, he'd told her the agreement between them would only ever be physical, but that was so he could make her accept the truth, accept the way they felt about each other. Without expectations, without letting her fear of attachment get in the way. He shoved his hands in his hair. But it wasn't her issues threatening to destroy their relationship before it began. It was him. His petty jealousy. His possessiveness. His inability to trust.

The two women in his life he should have been able to count on most, his mother and his wife, had lied and cheated. And he was now realizing the full effect those betrayals had had on him. How it had messed him up. That because of it, he didn't trust his own damn judgment, when he *knew* Alex would never do that to him.

If he didn't sort his shit out, he'd ruin everything. He'd lose Alex for good.

He shouldn't have let her walk out his apartment door. He should have held on to her and made her understand.

"Deacon?"

He turned to find Emily standing by her car. So preoccupied with Alex, he hadn't even seen it when he drove in. "What are you doing here?"

Her lip quivered. "I—I need to talk to you. Please don't tell me to go."

"We have nothing to discuss. Not a damned thing."

He turned away, but she rushed after him and grabbed his arm. "Please. I'm not doing so well, Deacon. I—I think I might do something stupid." A tear streaked down her perfectly made-up face. "I miss you so much. Seeing you with…" Her face twisted. "With *her*." She shook her head. "I can't bear it."

"What do you think you might do, Emily?" She shook her head again, and he grabbed her upper arms. "Answer me."

"I'm sorry. I'm so sorry," she sobbed, burying her face against his chest.

He had no choice but to hold her while she cried, when all he wanted to do was shake the shit out of her, beg her to leave him the fuck alone. This woman had screwed with his life, made him fucking miserable, and he was trapped, chained to her in a way that had him waking up at night in a cold sweat. He sure as hell wouldn't let her kill herself over him. That was something he could never live with. But no matter how many doctors and psychiatrists she saw, it always came back to this. Her obsession with him.

"Why aren't you with Steve?"

"He's away on business." She brushed her tears away.

"How would he feel if he knew you were here?"

She sucked in a breath and looked away. "I doubt he'd care." Her eyes, round and liquid, stared up at him. "He's not you."

Jesus Christ. "Come upstairs." She gave him a wobbly smile and clutched his hand like a lifeline. The thought made him want to throw up.

Emily had been doing great for the last eighteen months. It seemed like she'd finally moved on. Could he trust this? This sudden relapse? She'd manipulated him more times than he could remember. But then, how could he risk not believing her?

If he ignored her cry for help and something happened…

Shit.

He took her up to his apartment and let her in. "Take a seat. I'll make you some tea."

So fucking polite, so normal. *Have some nice, soothing tea while you emotionally blackmail me, while you keep me away from the only woman I've ever loved.*

He leaned against the counter and took several steadying breaths. Jesus, could he be any more of an asshole? For all he knew, Emily was suffering some kind of emotional breakdown. It wouldn't be the first he'd ridden out with her—but it sure as hell needed to be the last. He couldn't be her crutch, not anymore. He needed to talk her into getting help.

He pulled out the cups and glanced at his watch. *Dammit.*

There was no way he'd make his dinner meeting tonight, but more frustrating, he doubted he'd get to see Alex. He quickly called about dinner, made his apologies, and rescheduled, then scrolled down to Alex's name. The phone rang for so long he started to think she wouldn't answer.

. "Hello."

The sound of her voice went a long way to soothing the stress and anxiety he always felt when Emily was like this. "Hey."

The pause before she spoke, that hint of wariness, fucking twisted him up inside. "Worried I'm not coming?"

"No, I—"

"We have a deal, right?"

Deal. It wasn't a fucking deal, not to him. And as much as she tried to deny it, she knew it, too. "Alex…"

"We still have a deal, don't we, Deacon?" There was an acerbic bite to her voice—her tone damn near gave him frostbite. He knew she was still angry after the way he'd behaved this morning—she had every right to be—but he got the feeling this was something more.

He held the phone tighter to his ear. "Talk to me, Alex. I know I—"

"I'm getting dressed. I'll head over to your place when I'm ready."

Her voice was still cold, but she'd dropped the quietly controlled anger. Now she just sounded emotionless, distant. Fuck. She was holding back, keeping her feelings locked down, and he hated it.

"Deacon?" Emily's voice drifted in from the hall and, he was positive, bounced off the kitchen cabinets and right down the goddamn receiver to Alex.

"You still at work?" Alex asked.

"Look, something's come up. I, ah...I have to cancel our plans for tonight." He wanted to say more, so much more, but Emily chose that moment to walk into the kitchen.

Alex was silent for several seconds, then she laughed, the sound forced, distant. "Jesus. You're so damn predictable."

Goddammit. "No. Listen to me—"

Emily's face crumpled. "Are you...are you talking to her?"

After the way things had been left between them, this was the last thing he needed. Alex barely trusted him as it was. With the scratches and the confrontation in the store... She'd jump to the wrong conclusion without doubt. His little viper would use it as another way to protect herself, an excuse to push him away, and he couldn't have that. He was doing a good enough job of that on his own.

"I have to go. I'm sorry." He wanted to tell her about Emily—all of it, the lies, the betrayal—but the memory of his ex sitting in the bathtub the day after he'd found her in bed with another man, a blade to her wrist and swearing she'd cut her vein wide open if he exposed her, if he told her family and friends what she'd done to keep him—stopped him cold. She couldn't bear the humiliation. All she had left was her position in society. She'd lost him, if she lost that, too…

He couldn't risk it, couldn't risk telling anyone, not even Alex.

Alex cleared her throat. "Yeah, sure."

Dread slammed him hard. "This morning, I…" He glanced up at Emily, and those cold blue eyes were locked on him. "I'll talk to you soon, okay?"

"Forget it, Deacon. I have," Alex said, then hung up.

• • •

Alex rolled an old tire around the side of the garage to stash behind the building. Really, this job could wait till later, but she needed a minute. Rusty had been watching her all damn day, and Piper just flat-out wouldn't leave her alone. They weren't blind. They knew something was up. Something she could never tell them.

And being a crabby bitch all day hadn't helped, either.

I'll talk to you soon, okay?

Those words kept running through her mind. If that wasn't a kiss-off, she didn't know what was. One minute he missed her, couldn't get enough of her, the next, she was finding lipstick-stained shirts in his trash and he couldn't get away fast enough. She shoved down the stab of pain. Her feelings didn't matter in all this. He'd made that clear from the start.

All that mattered now was what this meant for West

Restoration.

Lifting the tire, she stacked it on top of the others, then turned to leave and slammed up against a hard chest.

She opened her mouth to scream bloody murder, but a hand slapped over her mouth—and Deacon filled her vision. "It's just me."

She yanked his fingers away. "What do you think you're doing?" Then without conscious thought, her gaze moved over him, ate up every inch of his body. It had only been a day, but it felt like forever. So many emotions pounded through her, making her dizzy. She didn't know whether to punch him or kiss the living daylights out of him.

"I had to come and see you." He moved in, crowded her, pressed her into the warm steel wall of the garage at her back. "Last night…something came up."

His back muscles tensed under her hands, and she realized she'd wrapped herself around him instinctively. That brought her up short.

Wise the hell up, Alex.

His dark gaze zeroed in on her mouth. If he kissed her right now, she'd be lost. "You don't owe me an explanation. You've been busy with your suit buddies, whatever." She shoved at his chest to get some space and shrugged. "Hey, I get it. Whores and five-star restaurants don't mix, right?"

Suddenly his hands were on her ass, and she was up against the wall. He shoved her higher, so they were eye level, and that big hard body pressed into hers. His solid thighs were wedged between hers, forcing her to open for him, and he ground the hard ridge of his erection against her center. The delicious pressure had her crying out. Then he stepped back from the wall suddenly, taking her with him.

Just long enough for one of those big hands to leave her butt and come down again on the same cheek with a loud *smack*.

Heat hit her face, anger and—dammit—lust firing her blood. She fought to get free, but he just pressed into her harder.

"You're not going anywhere. You are not running away. You will listen to me." She turned away, but he grabbed her chin, using his hips to hold her where he wanted her, and made her look at him. "I didn't go to the dinner meeting... something else came up. Something that kept me from you." He cursed under his breath. "I don't give a damn about five-star restaurants, and if you call yourself a whore once more, just once, I'll put you over my knee."

"You wouldn't dare." She tried to shove him back, but he didn't budge.

Heat flashed behind his eyes. "Try me."

Her lower belly clenched at his words, remembering the way he'd spanked her over her kitchen table, and she barely resisted rubbing up against that scorching-hot flesh still pressed between her thighs. "So what? We're still doing this?" She bit her lip, hated the strain in her voice, the need he had to have heard. *Idiot.*

He squeezed her ass. "I just need a couple days. That's all. I have... There's something I need to finalize, something that requires my entire focus. Believe me, no one will be happier than me when it's over."

She wanted to question him further, ask him about the shirt in his bathroom. Tell him what an asshole he'd been, that she didn't deserve to be treated that way. But he chose that moment to bury his face against her throat and scrape his teeth against her skin, nipping then sucking away the sting, and the words got stuck in her throat.

"I've been going out of my mind, baby."

He ground against her again, and she moaned, circling her hips, reaching for the release that was already so close just from having him pressed against her. God, she was pathetic, weak. She let her head fall back against the warm steel behind her in an attempt to ground herself, to regain some common sense. But her body didn't give a flying fuck about common sense—it cried out to have him inside her again.

"Say you'll wait, Alex. Say that you'll give me a couple days."

Right then, she couldn't remember her own name, let alone the reasons this wasn't a good idea. All her doubts were dissolving into a puddle at his feet. Then his mouth was on hers, and she was burning from the inside out. His tongue met hers, and she felt each sensual slide, each wild thrust between her quivering thighs. The world vanished around her. Her body didn't want anything to do with logic, it wanted Deacon, his hands, his mouth, his cock inside her.

He pulled back, kissing her jaw, her neck, that spot below her ear. "I'm sorry," he whispered. Her chest squeezed. Yeah, she was still pissed, hurt after what happened, the way he'd acted, but maybe... "For canceling our plans. God, I missed you."

What? She froze. His words were like a bucket of ice water dumped on her head.

No "sorry for doubting you, for believing you could be sleeping with someone else behind my back." No "sorry for letting you walk away and making you feel like the worthless whore that asshole had mistaken you for." And no explanation for the time he suddenly needed or why there was a shirt in his bathroom covered in pink goddamn lipstick.

She shoved his shoulders, hard. "That's what you're sorry for? You can't think of anything else? Nothing?"

"Alex…"

"Jesus, you really are nothing but a self-centered asshole, aren't you?"

He'd stilled but kept his arms around her, not letting her push him away. "Talk to me, don't fucking push me away, and don't shut me out."

Shut him out? He was the one keeping secrets and acting like a jerk.

This might be nothing but a business deal to him, but it wasn't to her, not anymore. She'd tried to keep her emotions out of it, but she'd failed, miserably. There was no point denying it anymore. She wanted what he would never give her.

Deacon had been ashamed of her. So ashamed the woman he'd been seen out with over the last two weeks had been pegged as some high-class call girl that he'd canceled their dinner plans to avoid more embarrassment. He could give her all the excuses he wanted, but that was the real reason. To him, she would never be good enough. And that hurt. A lot.

The couple of days he needed were more than likely to cover his ass, in case the asshole Deacon had assaulted spilled his guts and all the nice people he'd introduced her to as his date thought they'd been breaking bread with Deacon's whore.

The expression on his face when he'd let her walk out of his apartment was stuck in her head.

She'd given him a chance, an opening to admit he cared, and he hadn't taken it. Because he didn't feel that way about her. All he felt for her was lust. She was good enough to fuck, but only when it didn't get in the way of business.

And she'd stupidly gone to him that morning, ready to spill her guts, to yak up all the feelings she'd kept locked in her heart for so long. She'd trusted him. Something she didn't do lightly.

"Let me go." He didn't, he held on tighter.

"Talk to me."

She shoved at his shoulders. "I said let me the fuck go."

Every muscle in his body turned to stone beneath her hands. "Jesus. Alex…"

"We're done."

He flinched. "What?"

"I said we're done. Now back the hell up." She planted her hands on his shoulders and shoved again.

"You don't mean that. We have a—"

"Don't you *dare* say it." She shoved again, hands shaking, stomach twisting.

He finally released her, taking a step back. And dammit, she missed him instantly. "Talk to me, Alex."

She held his wild gaze, heart pounding. It suddenly hurt to even look at him. "If you try to force this, this messed-up arrangement, I will tell your sisters. You'll lose them, Deacon, and you know it. As for the business, word about the place is spreading. We've had several big jobs come in this week alone, and we're getting calls and doing quotes for more every day. So your excuse to sell this place, that we're playing shop, has been shot to shit."

"Alex," he growled, fists clenching and unclenching at his sides. "Would you stop for a minute and let me explain? You don't understand—"

"Despite what you think of me, I do understand. I

understand perfectly." He tried to grab her, but she wrenched away, taking several steps back. "Don't touch me."

He shoved his hands in his hair. "Sweetheart, don't do—"

"Deke!" Piper's voice cut him off as she walked around the corner. "I didn't know you were stopping by."

Deacon's gaze didn't falter; those blazing green eyes remained locked on her. Shoving her hands in her pockets, she moved around him, ignoring the way he growled her name under his breath, and forced a smile.

"Well, I need to get back to work. I'll leave you two to catch up," Alex murmured and made her escape.

She saw him drive away a short time later.

• • •

The next day seemed to creep by at a snail's pace and wasn't made any easier by the constant barrage of calls and texts from Deacon. She'd turned her phone off in the end. No way was she ready to talk to him. She had no interest in whatever bullshit he had to say.

She was ecstatic when she could finally climb the stairs to her apartment and, after a long, hot shower, change into her pj's and veg on the couch. *I will not cry. Not over him. Not again.*

Flicking through the channels, she searched for a show that didn't have anything to do with love or sex or relationships of any kind. In the end she chose a gory horror flick. "No chance of any lovey-dovey stuff on that."

The door to her apartment crashed open just as she was settling in. Rusty, with Piper hot on her heels, stormed in, wearing matching pissed-off expressions. *They know.*

Rusty rounded the couch and slammed a newspaper on the coffee table. "Have you seen this shit?"

Alex followed her friend's finger, stabbing at a collection of pictures on the society pages. She blinked down at them, hoping she was having some screwed-up hallucination. *No.*

But she wasn't and there in black and white was Deacon—and Emily. Her stomach dropped to her feet.

The first couple photos were of the two of them walking into a restaurant, his hand resting on her lower back. The next showed them climbing into a cab together, and the last was the pair of them out in front of his building. But this had been taken in the morning. Emily was wearing the same dress she'd had on in the dinner shots. Deke's hair was wet, slicked back like he'd just gotten out of the shower, and Emily was wrapped around him, head pressed to his chest. They'd spent the night together.

I'm going to throw up.

"That's who I heard in the background when he phoned." She hadn't realized she'd said it out loud until Rusty grabbed her arm.

"When? How long has that bitch had her claws back in my brother?"

Alex shook her head, still stunned by the images in front of her. "I don't know. I just heard a female voice…I have no idea how long it's been going on."

"Why'd he call?" Piper asked behind her. "Did he say anything about Emily?"

She shook her head. "No. He called to see if we could fit his car in for a service." What else could she say? "We didn't talk about anything else."

Rusty screwed up the paper and fired it in the trash. "If

he's going to keep shit-tastic secrets like this, then the lazy prick can service his own damn car."

The pair talked for a while longer, but Alex barely heard a word they said.

How could she have been so blind? The scratches, the lipstick on the shirt. The female voice on the other end of the phone when he'd canceled their plans. All the signs had been there. She just hadn't wanted to believe them.

Did he still love Emily? Had he ever stopped? And why had he asked her to give him a couple days? Kissing her like he had when he was obviously getting back with his ex-wife—did he think he could keep her his dirty little secret? Have the best of both worlds?

Anger, hot and sharp, sliced through her, helping to dull the ache in her chest.

A hand landed on her shoulder. "Alex. What's wrong?" Piper slid down beside her, concern on her face. "Why are you crying?"

Was she?

"Ah, Christ." Rusty slumped down, taking her other side, and looked at her sister. "You were right. They're sleeping together."

"What?" Alex shook her head, breaking out in a cold sweat.

"Save it, girl." Rusty slung her arm around Alex's shoulders. "We've seen his car here. You two are as subtle as a pair of humping wildebeests." Rusty gave her an encouraging squeeze. "Start talking."

Piper patted her hand, but her expression was pure determination. "Now."

Chapter Nineteen

Deacon was surprised and—he'd never thought he'd say this—pleased to see Steve when he'd entered the charity gala earlier that night. The sooner he got this mess with Emily sorted out, the sooner he could tell Alex everything. Until he told her the truth, all of it, they couldn't move forward. She loved him. He had to believe that. He just hoped she'd give him a chance to explain—that she'd believe him when he did.

He didn't waste time and took up the vacant space beside the man in question, who was currently propping up the bar and nursing what looked like a glass of whiskey. The main part of the evening was over. Deacon had played his part, schmoozed the main players and listened to the never-ending speeches. The cause was extremely important to him, and something he intended to contribute to for the foreseeable future, but after what had happened with Alex the day before, the way she'd looked at him, like he'd cut her heart out and ground it into the asphalt, this wasn't where he wanted to be. He was anxious to get this over with, to go to her, to finally come clean.

He turned to Steve. "I wasn't expecting to see you here tonight."

The guy snorted. "I'll bet." He shook his head and swayed on his seat, quickly righting himself.

How was he supposed to have a reasonable discussion with the man when he was shitfaced, or close to it, anyway. "I've tried to call you several times, but for some reason you've been ignoring my calls."

He snorted again. "We have nothing to discuss."

Deacon tried not to grind his teeth. "Emily, for one."

"Don't mention that bitch's name to me."

"We need to—"

"She told me you'd moved her back in."

The blood in his veins turned to ice. "What?"

"I can't believe you took her back."

Took her back? "I haven't."

"That's not what she's saying."

"She convinced me she'd relapsed. That she might hurt herself."

Steve snorted. "Looks like she's played us both for a fool."

When the hell would he learn? He'd lied to Alex, been forced to stay away from her. Forced to suffer Emily in his home the last couple days because she'd convinced him—and he'd stupidly believed her—that she had nowhere else to go. He'd sat with her for hours, doing his best to convince her to get more help. She'd played the victim so well, while she slept in his fucking spare room. And all the while, she'd been plotting. Some sick attempt to get him back.

Steve took a sip of his drink. "I asked her to marry me. Did you know that? She turned me down. Apparently, I don't make enough money." He slammed the glass on the bar. "So fucking cold."

Deacon didn't reply, too stunned, too damn angry at himself for letting her do this to him, again. Steve took his silence as an invitation to keep talking.

"I'm surprised she didn't tell you during your cozy dinner date." Steve must have read the confusion on his face. "You two were plastered all over the society pages."

His first thought went to Alex, but he quickly brushed it aside. The only way she'd read the society pages was at gunpoint.

"She's made fools of us, both of us, right from the start."

Deacon turned to walk away. He needed to find Emily. He'd seen her when he'd walked in and had planned to avoid her all evening, but now he wanted to find her so he could wring her goddamn neck.

Steve grabbed his arm, stopping him. "Do you know why she slept with me that first time? Why you caught us? Because she wanted to make you jealous." He waved his hand around. "So you'd realize you loved her." He snickered. "Of course you ended things, and when her father found out that she'd lied to you about a pregnancy and screwed around with me, he cut her off."

What? "She told you about the baby?"

"Oh, no. No, no, no. She wouldn't risk scaring off her meal ticket. I heard her and Tammy talking. She was only with me until she could win you back, you see. Then you went and found someone else and blew Emily's plan all to hell. She thought it was only a matter of time before you forgave her for her lies, and then she'd lure you back."

She'd been manipulating him all this time. "The counseling sessions I've been paying for? The emotional breakdowns?"

"She never went to a session. The guy promised to keep his mouth shut if she...sorry, if *you* kept paying. The only thing wrong with Emily is that she's a money-hungry, manipulative bitch." He shook his head. "Nothing can fix that shit."

He spotted Emily across the room and pushed off the bar, determined to confront her. But then he noticed several people had stopped in their tracks, staring at something near the entrance.

Deacon saw Jarrod Prescott standing near the main doors, and he watched as a grin spread across the other man's face before he strode over to whoever was causing the commotion. Dread moved through him when he heard a very distinctive laugh. Rusty.

Then he saw them, his sisters and Alex, break through the crowd. All three were dressed like they were out clubbing— in other words, practically naked. Alex had on the boots he'd bought her and a skirt so short he knew if she turned around and leaned forward, he'd see ass cheek. He wanted to drag her out of there and give her the scene she'd come for, but she was doing a good job of it on her own.

Jarrod joined them, and the bastard slung his arm around Alex's shoulders, grinned, and whispered something in her ear. She looked up at him, threw her head back, and laughed.

He lost it.

By the time he'd pushed through the growing crowd,

Piper was sitting on the CEO of Tech Industries's lap, and Rusty had pulled the president of the biggest finance company in Miami up to dance. The guy was close to eighty and looked like he might stroke out at any moment.

He stopped in front of Alex, close to stroking out himself, especially if Prescott didn't take his goddamn hands off her. "You have it, you've got my attention."

The woman completely ignored him, still chatting it up with Jarrod fucking Prescott. He didn't care what others thought. He could never be anything but proud to be seen with Alex. It didn't matter to him what she wore, he'd still be the luckiest man in the world. What pissed him off was the fact *she* thought this would embarrass him.

"Alex."

Those dark eyes moved to him, locked on, daring him to blow his stack, to walk away, to prove her low opinion of him. She placed her hand on his chest, and he sucked in a breath just from her touch. "There you are, Daddy," she said looking up at him from beneath lowered lashes, a smirk on her face as she dragged a finger slowly down his abs to his belt buckle.

Jesus. Some of these people might be ignorant enough to believe that's what he was to her, a goddamn sugar daddy, but Alex—and his fucking sisters—should know him a hell of a lot better than that.

Jarrod chuckled, and Deacon shot him a dark look. The guy wisely removed his arm from around her shoulders.

Deacon grabbed Alex's arm, intending to take her somewhere more private, but she shook him off. "Take your hands off me." Her voice was deceptively calm, but he didn't miss the way it shook. It damn near killed him.

Those photos of him and Emily in the newspaper, Alex had seen them. He couldn't think of any other reason for this. "We need to talk. Those pictures—"

She crossed her arms, causing her barely covered breasts to almost pop out of her top. "The time for talk is over, Deke."

He shrugged out of his jacket. "Put this on. Now." Every male in the room had his eyes on her, on his woman, and he wanted to tear their fucking eyes out.

"Why? Are you ashamed to be seen with your whore? Afraid your *wife* will see us?"

He shoved a hand through his hair. "I don't have a wife, Alex. You know that."

Her beautiful face twisted—anger, hurt, it was all there to see. She hid nothing. She loved him. She loved him, and he'd hurt her. Badly. "Alex...sweetheart..."

Her hand connected with the side of his face, the sound loud in the now near silent room. "Don't call me that."

His sisters were at Alex's side in an instant. Rusty scowled at him. "You fucked up, Deke, big-time." Then she grabbed Alex's hand. "Come on. Let's get the hell out of here."

Then Piper, his usually cool-headed, sweet sister, stepped up to him. "If you bring that skank"—she pointed over his shoulder, and he knew Emily was standing right behind him, making this ten times worse, and as usual, taking advantage of the situation for her own gain—"to my cottage, I'll run the bitch down, then back over her for good measure."

Emily gasped, and he spun to face his ex-wife. "Walk away from me, now. Before I say something in front of all these people you sure as hell won't want me to."

She grabbed his arm, and he shook her off. "I love you, Deacon." She said it without an ounce of real emotion except desperation, desperation that had nothing to do with losing a man who was supposedly the love of her life.

"Well, that's unfortunate"—he turned back to the three pissed-off females still standing behind him—"because I'm in love with Alex." Alex's eyes widened, and his sisters' mouths dropped open. "Are you really so shocked?" he rasped. He heard Emily's broken sob behind him, heard her hasty retreat, but kept his gaze on Alex. "Baby?"

Alex stumbled back a step and shook her head, a tear streaking down her cheek, then she spun on her heel and ran from the room.

Rusty grabbed his arm when he started after her. "What about Emily, the photos?"

"I don't have time to explain."

Piper joined her older sister and crossed her arms. "Make time, or we'll make sure you never get near her again."

He was on the verge of losing his mind. Every second Alex was getting farther away from him. "There's nothing going on between me and Emily. She's been playing me, manipulating situations, like she always has. I love Alex."

"Bitch," Piper growled.

"You better make this right. You better do everything in your power to make our girl listen to you." Rusty's fierce expression wobbled. "You made her cry, Deke. Alex never cries. Ever. Not since—"

Not since she ran through a window at the cottage to avoid being taken back to her foster home. She'd gotten that wicked scar on her arm as a reminder. How could she ever forgive him? Alex had suffered more than her fair share of pain, and he'd done nothing but cause her more.

He had to get to her, make her understand. He took off running flat out through the room and onto the street.

But he was too late.

Alex was gone.

Chapter Twenty

Alex lay back on the couch and watched Richard Gere open a velvet-covered jewelry box, then snap it down on Julia Roberts's fingers. It was supposed to be some iconic, funny, unscripted part of this scene. In her opinion, it just made Edward look like a major jerk. *Here, desperate prostitute girl, look what I have for you.*

Snap.

Sucker! Wouldn't want you to forget your place now.

What a complete and utter asshole.

Her phone started up again. A picture of Deacon flashed on the screen. He was smiling. The one with his elusive dimple on display. *Speaking of assholes.* She hit end and cut off the call.

Groaning, she squeezed her eyes closed, trying to make her mind shut the hell up. *Nope, not working.* As hard as she tried, she couldn't get the look on his face out of her head, his words on constant loop, banging around her skull.

I'm in love with Alex.

She scrubbed her hands over her face. He didn't mean it. How could he?

Walking into that room, after seeing those pictures— the pain had been acute, so much so, she'd felt like she was floating outside her body, a bystander to her own pathetic life. But she'd refused to let him see how much his betrayal had broken her. Her only thought had been making him pay, humiliating him the way he had her. Making him hurt, too, the only way she knew how.

And then he'd said it, said he loved her, and she'd freaked out.

Deacon was probably still getting his balls served to him by his irate sisters. God, she hadn't meant to tell them, but seeing those pictures broke something inside her, and before she knew what she was doing, she'd spilled her guts. The last thing she wanted was to mess up Piper and Rusty's relationship with their brother.

Jesus, her head hurt.

Rolling off the couch, she climbed to her feet and dusted potato chip crumbs off her shirt. *Gah! What a mess.* And she wasn't just talking about the carpet. She looked down at her-self, still in the ridiculous outfit Rusty had shoved her in the previous evening. "What was I thinking?"

That was the problem—her brain hadn't been in the driver's seat.

Dragging her feet to the bathroom, she looked in the mirror. Mascara was smudged down her face, hair a tangled rat's nest. She was rocking the whole *Return of the Living Dead* look. Nice.

Clean yourself up, girl. Dust yourself off and keep moving forward. Jacob's voice echoed in her mind. He'd helped her through some of the worst times of her life. Made sure she didn't stumble and fall, no matter what obstacle was thrown in her way. It's what she did. She didn't know how to do anything else. If she stopped, let the pain take hold—stopped moving forward—she felt like she might turn to stone, might get back on the couch and never get off again.

She couldn't avoid her friends forever. Tomorrow morning cars would arrive at the garage, jobs that needed to be done. Time wouldn't stop because her heart was broken. She couldn't spend the rest of her life hiding from everyone.

She needed to talk to Deke.

He'd said he loved her, but she wouldn't, *couldn't* believe in it. Her feelings hadn't mattered when he'd gone back to his ex. He'd played them both. No one wanted to be the other woman. And that's what he'd made the both of them.

She had no love for Deacon's ex-wife, and she didn't know the cause of his and Emily's split, but the cold way he'd shut her down in front of that room full of people...no one deserved that, not even Emily.

He'd lied and he'd cheated. She still found it hard to believe. She knew Deacon was ruthless in the boardroom, but she'd never dreamed he could be just as ruthless with the people around him, the people who cared for him. He had two sisters he loved and respected. His actions made no sense.

Stop.

She slammed the brakes on the direction her thoughts were taking. There was no excuse for it. No matter how out of character it seemed, the proof was in black and white in a crumpled heap in her recycle bin.

After a long, hot shower, she pulled on her favorite baggy Led Zeppelin T-shirt and felt slightly more human. Finger combing her damp hair, she headed back to the living room. Sleep wasn't an option, not yet. Right then she thought she might never sleep again, because every time she closed her eyes, she saw him. Those intense green eyes, making her feel things she'd tried to deny—silently telling lies, making promises that meant nothing. Making her hope, making her believe in him.

Bang. Bang. Bang.

Alex jumped and spun around at the sound of a fist connecting with her door.

"Alex, get down to the workshop," Rusty called through the door. "Quickly!" That was followed by the sound of her friend's boots pounding back down the stairs. A surge of adrenaline shot though her veins. Was Piper hurt?

She didn't muck around, shoved her feet in her work boots, flung her door open, and ran down after her. When she pushed open the garage door the place was pitch-dark. Walking in, she groped for the lights. "Rusty? Piper? What's going on?"

The door banged shut behind her, followed by the sound of the lock engaging. "Hey!" She threw the switch, and the overhead lights blinked to life, making her squint against the harsh brightness. She tried the door. Locked. Those bitches had locked her in. She banged on the steel door. "Let me the hell out."

Nothing. Complete silence.

The sound of a car door opening behind her had her freezing on the spot.

No. They wouldn't, would they?

"Alex?"

Bitches!

Deacon's usually smooth, deep voice was a hell of a lot deeper than usual, and not as steady. She couldn't make herself turn around.

"Look at me, Alex, please?"

His voice was closer that time, but she remained rooted to the spot. "I don't want to," she whispered.

If I look at you, I'll break.

Then he was right behind her, his tight stomach, his chest, plastered against her back. She shivered as the heat of his body soaked through her thin T-shirt. His hands snaked around to rest on her belly, and he dropped his forehead to her shoulder. "Please, Alex." He nuzzled the side of her neck and sucked in a deep breath. "Please let me explain."

She rested her head against the cool steel in front of her, trying to fight the way her body reacted to his touch, how right it felt. With a strength she didn't know she possessed, she removed his arms from around her waist and stepped away. "There's nothing to say. Nothing that can change what's happened." She crossed her arms and shuffled a step to the side to get some much-needed space. "I saw the pictures, Deacon. I know about you and Emily. I know you're sleeping with her."

He shoved a hand in his hair, making it stick up on one side. She took him in. He looked like shit. Stubble darkened his jaw, and his eyes were bloodshot, like he'd had about as much sleep as she had. He was wearing the same trousers and shirt he'd had on at the charity event, only he'd lost the jacket and tie and the sleeves were rolled up to his elbows.

"There is no me and Emily." His eyes begged her to

believe him, and God, she wanted to, but how could she? "I haven't slept in the same bed with my ex-wife… I haven't had sex with my ex-wife since we were married, and that side of our relationship fizzled out after the first few months." He swallowed, throat working. "I'll understand if you choose to walk away after the lies, the secrets, the fucked-up way I went about everything, but I need to explain. Will you let me?"

Deacon had never talked about his marriage with Emily or the reason it fell apart, but she'd always wondered, had guessed it had to be something pretty bad for Deacon to be so closed off about it, especially with his sisters. "What happened?"

He released a shaky breath. "It's kind of hard to get a hard-on over a woman who lies about being pregnant to get you back, manipulating you into marrying her because she knows the pain and guilt you felt when your mother left… that because I'd opened my mouth, told my father what I'd seen, my sisters grew up without their mother. She knew I wouldn't want that for my own child." He shoved both hands in his pockets. "I told her, you see, about you and me."

Alex stood frozen, struggling to take it all in.

"She called that morning, the morning after you gave yourself to me." His voice shook on the last word, so much longing in his gaze, she struggled for breath. "I told her that she had to stop calling, that I was in love with you. She broke down, told me she was pregnant. After that, after she told me she was carrying my child…" He shook his head. "I didn't think I had any other choice. So I went back to her. And fuck, leaving you that day…it was the hardest thing I've ever done." His nostrils flared. "I found out months later there was no baby, never had been. I told her we were through."

Alex was stunned. How could Emily do that to him? Lie and scheme like that? "What happened?" she whispered.

"She threatened to kill herself if I left. If I told anyone what she'd done. Convinced me she'd fall apart if I didn't stay. I planned to leave when she was better, but every time I thought she was doing okay, that finally I could leave, she'd relapse. I was stuck in that nightmare for four years.

"Then I caught her in bed with Steve—another ploy, this time an attempt to make me jealous, to get our relationship back. It blew up in her face. I left."

"Oh my God." He'd been through hell because of that selfish bitch.

"It gets worse. I found out yesterday there's nothing wrong with her, there never was. She's been manipulating me all these years. Her family cut her off after what happened between us, and she was biding her time with Steve until I wised up and took her back. She used her fake illness to keep me tied to her." He held Alex's gaze. "But you threw a monkey wrench in the works and screwed up her plan to win me back. So she pulled the suicide card again. That's why I was with her, why I couldn't tell you what was going on. I was afraid what she'd do—that she'd harm herself. She gave me no other choice. I was trying to convince her to get the help I thought she needed."

He moved in then, brushing her hair over her shoulder, cupping the side of her neck, gently moving his thumb along her jaw. "I've loved you since that first time, Alex." He shook his head. "No. If I'm honest, long before then. But you were still so young, and I knew you weren't ready for what I wanted with you. Then I broke up with Emily, and as soon as I saw you again, I knew I had to have you, that I couldn't wait any longer."

Her head was spinning. *He loved her. He had always loved her.* "What about blackmailing me into your bed?"

"You don't trust easily, Alex, and I'd already hurt you. I didn't know how else to get you to give me another chance, to spend time with me, to let me love you like you deserved."

"You were never going to sell this place?"

He shook his head and pulled out his cell phone, opened his text messages, and showed her a reply from David Cannon.

Thanks for the referral. My car looks amazing.

"You sent Mr. Cannon to us?"

"No." He shook his head. "I referred him; the decision was his. I barely know the man, so this wasn't a favor to me. We aren't business associates. I just met him through a friend."

"He's not the first, is he?"

He shook his head. "I believe in you, in this place."

She sucked in a breath, the lump clogging her throat suddenly escaping on a giant sob. All the emotion she'd held back over the last few days—the last few years—came rushing forward. She had no hope of holding it back. She shook her head. "No Emily?"

"No Emily." He ran his thumb over her lower lip.

"And you…you love *me*?"

"Yes, I love you. So fucking much," he choked.

Her body started to tremble so hard her legs felt weak. He pulled her into his arms, hands going to her butt. He lifted her off the ground, and she wrapped her legs around his waist, arms circling his neck. Hot tears streamed down her face and soaked into his shirt.

He kissed the top of her head. "I know I went about this all the wrong way, and I've acted like a jealous, overbearing asshole, but I promise you this—it stops now, baby. You didn't deserve any of it. I let my past get in the way of our future. I won't let that happen again."

She tightened her arms around his neck. "I'm not your mom, and I'm not Emily, Deke," she choked. "I would never hurt you like that. Ever."

"I know, baby."

She vaguely felt him move. Heard him kick the door, tell Rusty to open up. Then they were going up the stairs to her apartment, and the next thing she knew, Deacon was lowering her onto her bed.

She'd been so damn blind, had turned Deacon into some kind of power-hungry monster in her head. All to protect herself from the truth, a truth she'd been too afraid to face. She'd acted like a coward, had pushed him away all those months ago instead of taking a risk, afraid to love, to be loved in return.

But she'd known, deep down under all the baggage, the pain she hid behind, she'd known that Deacon would never hurt her, would never do anything to hurt his sisters. She knew this because she knew him.

And because of three magical, wonderful words.

Deacon loved her.

Chapter Twenty-One

Deacon removed her boots, letting them fall to the floor. Crawling up the mattress, he came down on top of her. It felt so good to have her beneath him. He'd been craving this, being able to touch her, feel her warm, smooth skin beneath his fingers. She felt small, almost fragile right then, and he slid his arms around her, holding her to him.

Jesus, he couldn't believe she was giving him another chance, that she was finally his.

"Alex?" Her body shook, and her eyes were screwed shut, big fat tears rolling down her cheeks. She was killing him. "Baby…" He tried to brush away her tears but more replaced them instantly. "Sweetheart, please don't cry… What can I do? How can I make it better?"

"Kiss it b-better," she sobbed.

Her legs were wrapped around his waist, and he became aware of the heat between her thighs, the way she was flush against his abs, scalding him through her panties. He groaned. "You want me to kiss it better?"

"Y-yes."

She wiggled beneath him, and he chuckled. "Where do you want your kiss?" He lifted up and dragged her T-shirt higher, revealing her taut belly. Leaning down, he licked and sucked the smooth skin, holding her immobile when she wiggled harder. Trailing hot kisses across her ribs, he moved the shirt higher. "What about here?"

She moaned softly when he wrapped his lips around a peaked nipple and gently sucked. She smelled of arousal and the vanilla soap she used, and something more, something purely Alex. His cock throbbed against his zipper, starving for more, desperate to get inside her. He kissed and sucked, then moved to the other side, to that sexy purple bar piercing her perfect little nipple, tonguing it gently, making her writhe and gasp.

"You like that?" He blew on her damp flesh, cursing under his breath when she lifted her hips, rubbing herself against his stomach.

Fingers threading through his hair, she pulled the strands at the same time, holding him to her. "Harder," she whimpered.

He did as she asked, sucking harder and tugging gently until her hips were thrusting against him. "You want to come, sweetheart?"

"Yes. Please, Deacon."

He'd gotten a glimpse of her like this, so beautifully vulnerable, unguarded, when he'd made love to her in the garage, but he'd never seen her this way, this open, this free of restraint. She took his breath away, humbled him. "You're so beautiful." He dragged her shirt up and over her head, needing her completely bared to him, then slid her panties down her legs. She reared up, tugged at the buttons of his shirt, and he took over, yanking it over his head, then made quick work of the rest of his clothes.

When he covered her again, he groaned at the feel of her bare skin against his. Her legs wrapped around his hips, and she ground against him. *Jesus.* He was hanging on by a goddamned thread.

Sliding a hand up the side of her neck, fingers sinking into her dark, silky hair, he took her mouth, kissing her like he'd wanted to the minute she walked into the garage. She returned his kiss, wild and hungry, rubbing herself against him, gasping into his mouth. Alex was almost frantic in her need, desperate for him. He loved it, loved her like this. Loved her. And as much as he wanted to hold her down, take charge, pound out all the frustration, the hurt he'd caused her, he knew what she needed.

Wrapping his arms around her, he rolled to his back. Her hands immediately went to his cock, fisting him, positioning herself over him. "That's it, Alex, take it." Her hands landed on his shoulders, and she sank down hard. Jesus, she was slick and hot, and wrapped around him so tight he was close to losing it. Flinging her head back, she cried out, hips undulating in a way that made him hiss through gritted teeth. "Take what you need, baby. I'm all yours. I've always been yours."

The tears had slowed, but another sob broke past her swollen lips. Her fingers flexed, nails biting into his skin when she ground down hard, making them both moan. Then her eyes finally opened, those sexy, exotic eyes still glistening from her tears holding his. She didn't speak, just held his gaze as she moved on top of him, taking what she needed.

The woman was beautiful. Completely bare. Dark hair, wild around her shoulders. She took his breath away. But it was her eyes that held him transfixed—they hid nothing, gave him everything, showed him everything. He slid his hands up her thighs, gripped her hips, and thrust up into her. "Say you're mine, Alex. Say it."

Her movements grew frantic, her breathing erratic, skin flushed with her fast-approaching climax. He felt her tighten around him and slid his thumb up and over her clit, massaging the tight bud. "I'm not going anywhere, sweetheart. Ever. I promise you that."

Her lips trembled.

"Say it," he whispered.

"Yours. I'm yours," she cried, then threw her head back, screaming his name as she came.

He didn't take his eyes off her, not when his balls drew tight, and not when his own release tore through him, turning him into nothing but a gasping, shaking mess beneath her.

He didn't know how long they lay there afterward, her body draped over his, her breath tickling his throat with every exhale. He threaded his fingers though her hair and waited. Waited for her to process everything he'd said, to allow it to sink in. He wasn't going anywhere. Alex was his.

Finally she lifted her head and looked down at him. "So, you and me, huh?"

He couldn't read her expression. "Yep."

"No arrangement, no blackmail. Just…you and me."

"Uh-huh."

She lowered her head back to his chest, quiet again. After several minutes, he gave her hair a tug. "You got something to add to that?" His heart felt like it was pounding in his throat, damn near choking him.

When she lifted up again, she was grinning. "Oh, did I forget something?"

"You damn well know you did." He gave her ass a light slap.

She tapped her finger against her lip. "Let me see. Oh, I know... Yes, Deacon, you *are* a stud machine in the sack." Her grin got wider. "Better?"

"Don't mess with me, woman, not after the last couple days. Now say it, or I'll be forced to punish you." He flipped her onto her back and stared down at her. "I need to hear you say the words." He knew he sounded desperate, needy as hell, but that was because he was.

Her grin faded, and her eyes grew serious. She cupped his face in her hands and held his gaze. "Deacon West, I have loved you since I was fourteen years old. That has never changed, can never change. I will always love you. Always."

He sucked in a breath. "Jesus." Then, groaning, he buried his face against her throat. She rubbed his back while he pulled himself together enough to talk. But when he lifted up again, he couldn't find the words. There weren't any to express what he felt in that moment, so he kissed her, pouring everything he felt into that kiss. And when she wrapped her legs around his hips, urging him to take her again, he didn't think he had ever been—could ever be—happier. He sank inside her and made love to his woman, reassuring her, loving her the way he knew she needed.

"You and me," he whispered into her hair.

Epilogue

Alex's bare skin felt flushed, and not just from the sun's heat beating down. Deacon kissed his way up to the sensitive skin below her ear. "You hungry?"

She brushed her fingers through his hair, away from his forehead, and grinned. "Starving."

"I better feed you then." Taking her hands, he helped her into a sitting position on the hood of his father's Pontiac, his thighs still between hers. He took a step back, then stopped, head tilting to the side. "Wait, don't move…just, stay like that for a second."

"Why?" She darted a glance down at herself. "Is there a bug on me or something?"

He shook his head, laughter dancing in his gorgeous green eyes. "No. I'm memorizing the way you look right now, locking it away in my mind. Recently fucked, sitting on the hood of the Pontiac, sun lighting up that amazing golden skin, while the breeze ruffles your hair." He rubbed his hand over his mouth. "Beautiful doesn't cut it, Alex."

She swallowed hard, emotion clogging her throat. "You don't look too shabby yourself, Mr. CEO." Bare chest, jeans still undone, sweat glistening his skin, hair mussed from her fingers tugging on it. "Like someone just rocked your world," she teased.

Deacon had surprised her when she woke, telling her they were going on a picnic. As soon as he'd driven Jacob's old car out of the garage, she knew what he had in mind. The fantasy he'd told her about four months ago. It felt like such a long time ago now, when she'd been so afraid of her feelings, afraid to love him. But Deke made it easy. The guy wasn't hard to love.

"You rock my world every damn day just by being in it." He moved back in close, tugged down her skirt, and lifted her to the ground. Then, taking her hand, he led her over to the picnic blanket he had laid out by the lake. The area was completely secluded, idyllic, peaceful.

She stood there and looked out across the water. "It's so beautiful."

His fingers slipped around hers. "Yeah, I've never seen anything more stunning."

She turned back. His voice had gone incredibly deep, and he was staring up at her, already kneeling on the blanket. She tried to climb down beside him, but he stopped her. "Just stand there for me."

"What?" He reached into his pocket and pulled out a small velvet box. "Deacon…"

"Alex…"

"Shit," she breathed.

He chuckled nervously and licked his lips, fingers tightening around her now trembling ones. "You are the most amazing woman I've ever met. You're tough, loyal—God, incredibly sexy. But you're much more than that. I'm so thankful you let me in, trusted me with your heart." He took a shuddering breath. "I want to spend the rest of my life with you." He pressed a kiss against the inside of her wrist, and she struggled to breathe. "Alexandra Maria Franco, will you marry me?"

Her already weak knees just kind of gave out from underneath her, and she sank down in front of him, her vision blurred. "Yeah. Shit. Yes, I'll marry you."

He pulled her in tight, hand cupping her face, and kissed her hard and deep. "I'll make you happy, baby. I promise."

"You make me happy every day." She was crying freely, happy tears. She'd done that more than once in the last few months. Before Deacon had forced his way back into her life, she hadn't believed this kind of joy was even possible. That she would ever have this. But he proved her wrong every day. There was so much emotion on his handsome face, his love for her open and honest.

He smiled wide, the one that showed off that sexy dimple. "You know what this means, right?"

Sniffing, she buried her face in his neck, but he pulled her back up, wiping the tears from her cheeks. "The girls will be pissed that you're stealing me away from them." She chuckled. "You can tell them, but wait till I'm long gone." Of course she was joking. Rusty and Piper couldn't be happier for the both of them.

"I'm sure they'll get over it. I want you waking up in my

bed every morning. No more of this living in two different apartments." He lay back on the blanket and pulled her onto his chest. "They'll still get to see you every day, then you can come home to me every night."

Going up onto her elbow, she stared down at him. "I like the sound of that." Then she leaned in and kissed him. "Now how about a replay of that fantasy of yours?"

His gaze darkened. "I'm yours to command. Always."

Acknowledgments

First, to my husband and two children, thank you for putting up with me. And for the tea and chocolate deliveries! I love you guys.

To my editor, Karen Grove, thank you for your encouragement and support and the hard work you put into making this book the best it can be.

To Nicola Davidson, my friend and critique partner. As always, you are the wind beneath my wings!

To Mel Cryer, my amazing beta reader, thank you for always being excited to read one of my books.

To Tracey Alvarez, for the sprints, tireless encouragement, and moral support!

And last, but no means least, to my sister, Kelly, for suffering through the daily one-sided phone calls and being one of my biggest cheerleaders.

About the Author

Sherilee Gray lives in beautiful New Zealand with her husband and their two children. When she isn't writing, she spends her time reading, hoarding books, and eating copious amounts of chocolate.

Connect with Sherilee via Facebook, Twitter, her newsletter, or through her website www.sherileegray.com.

CPSIA information can be obtained
at www.ICGtesting.com
Printed in the USA
LVOW04s1321020516
486303LV00023B/208/P

9 781943 336470